Hannah Coulter

Also by Wendell Berry

FICTION
Fidelity
Jayber Crow
The Memory of Old Jack
Nathan Coulter
A Place on Earth
Remembering
That Distant Land
Watch With Me
The Wild Birds
A World Lost

POETRY
The Broken Ground
Clearing
Collected Poems: 1957–1982
The Country of Marriage
Entries
Farming: A Hand Book
Findings
Openings
A Part
Sabbaths
Sayings and Doings
The Selected Poems of Wendell Berry (1998)
A Timbered Choir
The Wheel

ESSAYS
Another Turn of the Crank
The Art of the Commonplace
Citizenship Papers
A Continuous Harmony
The Gift of Good Land
Harlan Hubbard: Life and Work
The Hidden Wound
Home Economics
Life Is a Miracle
Long-Legged House
Recollected Essays: 1965–1980
Sex, Economy, Freedom and Community
Standing by Words
The Unforeseen Wilderness
The Unsettling of America
What Are People For?

WENDELL BERRY

Hannah Coulter

A Novel

Shoemaker S&H Hoard *Washington, D.C.*

This book is a work of fiction. Nothing is in it that has not been imagined.

Library of Congress Cataloging-in-Publication Data
Berry, Wendell, 1934–
Hannah Coulter : a novel / Wendell Berry.
p. cm.
ISBN 1-59376-036-1
1. Port William (Ky. : Imaginary place)—Fiction.
2. Women—Kentucky—Fiction.
3. Kentucky—Fiction I. Title.
PS3552.E75H36 2004
813'.54—dc22   2004013121

Jacket and text design by David Bullen Design
Map and genealogy designed by Molly O'Halloran
Genealogy prepared by David S. McCowen

Printed in the United States of America

S͞H̠ Shoemaker & Hoard
A Division of Avalon Publishing Group, Inc.
Distributed by Publishers Group West

10 9 8 7 6 5 4 3 2 1

This book is given in gratitude
to Tanya Amyx Berry

Contents

Have drawn at last from time which takes away
And taking leaves all things in their right place
An image of forever
One and whole.

Edwin Muir

Part I

1

The Story Continuing

"I picked him up in my arms and I carried him home."

So Nathan would end the last of the stories of his childhood as he told it to our children.

This was in 1940. Nathan was sixteen. He and Jarrat, his dad, his dad's brother, Burley, and his grandpa Dave—the three of them had gone down into the river bottom, taking a team and wagon, to help a neighbor put up hay.

It was hot weather, "hay weather," the last of July. Dave Coulter, whom I too learned to call "Grandpa" though I never knew him, was eighty years old, no longer much use for work. While the younger men loaded and hauled in and unloaded the hay, Grandpa Coulter puttered about, or sat in the shade and slept, or carried water to the others when they needed a drink. Toward the middle of the afternoon he had one of the sick spells that he called "miseries," and Jarrat told Nathan, "Walk home with him. Help him along. Take care of him."

The two of them went up the hill together, stopping often. When they had got almost home, Grandpa staggered and went down, and couldn't be wakened. Nathan was a big boy by then, strong, and he gathered Grandpa into his arms and carried him the rest of the way up to the house where Grandma Coulter, whom I do remember a little, hurried to open the door and to make a place to lay him down.

Nathan thought of that, I am pretty certain, as the last day of his boy-hood. Past that day he told no more stories about himself. From then on he was in his own estimate and in his deeds a man who lived and worked as a man with his dad and his uncle Burley, expecting to go on working in the same place at the same work for the rest of his life. His older brother, Tom, had left home, but Nathan wanted to stay. He had not thought of going away or, yet, of marrying.

But then, pretty soon, the war came. Tom and then Nathan were called into the army. Tom was killed as the fighting passed up through Italy. Andy Catlett went there years later and found his grave. It was in a valley not far outside of Florence, a field of white crosses, row after row, gathered in the quiet.

Nathan didn't "cross the waters," as they used to say here, until the spring of 1945. And then he went pretty straight into the Battle of Oki-nawa, and lived, and was unhurt, and came home.

But his stories about himself stopped at the death of Grandpa Coulter. He would tell our children the stories of his childhood, mostly of the things he and Tom had done. They did a lot of things, and saw and went through a lot of things, some funny and some sad enough.

All I know of Tom Coulter I know of him as a boy in those stories Nathan told. Of Tom as a grown young man, as a soldier killed in the war far from Port William and forever gone, nobody spoke. I knew they didn't speak of him as they last knew him, living and so near his death, because they couldn't. And I understood why. They had got into the habit of silence because for too long after he died they couldn't talk about him without weeping out loud. And so he lives on now in my mind as a boy in old stories told to children.

Of Nathan himself, from the time when he and Tom roved about and played and worked together as boys, until after the war—when I turned aside from grief for the husband I had, who also was lost in the war, and finally could love Nathan and marry him—I know, beyond what I have learned to imagine, almost nothing.

He was, anyhow, a quiet man who never had much extra to say. He had stories enough, about Burley and Big Ellis and Tol Proudfoot and others, mostly funny. But about himself, about the coming of the war and his time in it, though he would say something occasionally, not much, not often, he told no stories. If the subject came up, he was apt to say, "Ignorant boys, killing each other," or something else about that short. And then, looking away, he would shake his head and say no more. Over the years I heard him say enough to know he didn't like the power of some people to say whether other people will live or die. He didn't like the idea of killing women and old men and children, or of destroying the world in order to kill people, or of great machines made only to kill people. What he did and what happened to him in the war, I don't know. While he was alive I couldn't ask him. After he was dead I learned what I could, and more than I could easily bear to know, about the Battle of Okinawa where he fought.

His story after the war, and especially after 1948, I know because it is my story too. It is our story, for I lived it with him. It is the story of our place in our time: our farm of "150 acres more or less," as the deed says, on the ridges and slopes above the creek known as Sand Ripple that runs down from Port William to the river. Nathan bought it in that year of 1948, hoping I would marry him, or in case I would, thinking he would need a place of his own to take me to.

Our story is the story of our place: how we married and came here, moved into this old house and made it livable again while we lived in it; how we raised our children here, and worked and hoped and paid the mortgage, and made a pretty good farm of a place that had been hard used and then almost forgotten; how we continued, making our life here day by day, after the children were gone; how we kept this place alive and plentiful, seeing it always as a place beyond the war—Nathan seeing it, as I now think, as if from inside a fire; how we got old, and Nathan died, and I have remained on for yet a little while to see how such lives as ours and such a place may fare in a bad time.

This is the story of my life, that while I lived it weighed upon me and pressed against me and filled all my senses to overflowing and now is like a dream dreamed. So close to the end now, what do I look forward to? "Today shalt thou be with me in paradise." Some morning, I pray, I'll have the good happiness of "the man who woke up dead," who Burley Coulter used to tell about.

This is my story, my giving of thanks.

2

A Steadman

I was a Steadman from up in the ridges behind Hargrave. Dalton and Callie were my parents, and I was their only child. We lived on a rough farm that had belonged, since my grandfather's death, to my grandmother. My father, her youngest son, farmed it as her tenant. We lived with my grandmother in her house, an old farmhouse of the usual kind: four rooms in front, divided upstairs and down by a wide hall, with another four rooms in an ell at the back. The farm had built the house but in those hard times was unable to maintain it. It was bare-boned and paintless, the weatherboard bleached and rain-stained. In places the stones of the foundation had sprawled from under the sills. The tall rooms were wonderfully cool in summer, but in the winter they were drafty and hard to heat. On windy days you could sit right by the stove and your back would be cold.

My grandmother was Arvinia Steadman. I called her "Grandmam." She was good to us, and all of us got along. She and my mother shared the housework, and they helped my father with the farmwork too when they were needed, like most farm women. We would all be at work together, sometimes with neighbors, in the plantbeds in the spring, in the harvest times of summer and fall, and in the stripping room in the winter. We worked hard, before day to after dark, and I helped and had my own jobs to do from the time I was five or six years old. The times were hard, and they got worse. I was seven when the Depression hit and eight in the terribly dry summer of 1930 when we drove the stock two miles to water.

It was a hard time, and most people now, if they could even imagine it, would say we were living a hard life. But there was understanding among us, we were never hungry, and we had good neighbors. I was mostly happy, or I certainly thought I was, until I was twelve years old.

The year I was twelve my mother died. She took the flu and then pneumonia, and then, almost before we could think that she might die, she was dead. By her grave, when we brought her there, there was a heap of snow on one side and a heap of dirt on the other.

And so I learned about grief, and about the absence and emptiness that for a long time make grief unforgettable. We went on, the three of us remaining, as we had to do. In all the practical ways we managed fine. Grandmam was still a vigorous woman, as she would be for years yet. My father, though seriously damaged by his loss for a while at least, was capable and a master of making do. I was big enough then to do a woman's part, and I did it. But we had a year when even to look at one another would make us grieve.

After about a year my father married again. That, it turned out, was not the best solution to his problem, and it took me from loss and grief into trouble of another kind. He married Ivy Crutchlow, a widow from our neighborhood. There is no use in dwelling on old ills, and I'm long past my grudge, but I have to say that she was not a good wife to my father, and she lived up to the bad reputation of stepmothers. The problem between Ivy and me was that she had two boys, Elvin and Allen, two and three years younger than I was, who were the stars in her crown, as she liked to tell you. They were all she had lived for since the death of their father, so it is understandable that she loved them entirely and didn't have any affection left over for me. She saw me as competition for them and, since we had little enough to spare of anything, she was always needing to take their side. She was always in a panic to see that they got enough, or their share, or, if she could work it, the best. If my grades in school were better than theirs, which they were, she would act as if I had got more than my share of a limited supply of good grades. Whatever she gave them seemed to her to be something she took away from me, even when it wasn't. And she couldn't hide her pleasure in such victories, even when she knew I didn't want whatever she had given them.

What was worse was that Elvin and Allen, set at odds with me already by their mother's preference, went about snooping and spying on me with a gleeful dirty-mindedness that I hated. I never had hated anybody before, but to find them creeping around after I came out of the privy, or giggling at the mere sight of my underwear on the clothesline, made me want to kill them.

My father, I suppose, had too much trouble of his own to be much aware of mine. His marriage to Ivy was as big a mistake for him as it was for me, and I think he found it out pretty quick. He was a humorous, good-natured man, maybe because he hoped for little and expected less and took his satisfactions where he found them. He got along with Elvin and Allen by joking and cutting up with them. He called them Scissor Lips and Bigwig. Though their mother spoiled them and did everything for them, they paid no attention to her at all, but they minded my father and did the work he set for them to do. Still, it was a divided, unhappy household we had then, and I know he felt it.

"She's going to prove out to be righter than everybody in this world, and she'll be the only one in Heaven—except, I reckon, for Elvin and Allen." That was the only comment my father ever made to me about Ivy. Mostly he dealt with her too by joking, and by staying out of the house as much as he could. Their failure was something you felt rather than saw.

The worst I saw of it was the night my father joined the church. There was a revival, and we were going every night to the white church that sat with the graveyard behind it at the edge of our little crossroads settlement of Shagbark.

It was good to sit there with everybody in the lighted church and to sing and listen to the preaching while the katydids cried in the warm night beyond the opened windows. What my father had done to be particularly repentant of, I don't know. He had done something.

The sermon was over and we were singing,

Just as I am, without one plea . . .

As soon as I saw that my father had stepped out into the aisle and started down to where the preacher stood, I knew it had something to do with

Ivy. They had quarreled, maybe. He was offering himself to God as an offering to Ivy. Or having proved in some way unacceptable to Ivy, he was hoping to be acceptable to God.

As the singing went on, he stood in front of us all with tears shining on his face. After the final prayer, when the people went to speak to him and shake his hand, Ivy ought to have gone too. Grandmam went and I went, but Ivy didn't go.

The trouble was that by dividing herself from him, Ivy somehow divided him from Grandmam and me. And what must have been clear enough to the two of them was forever a mystery to us. I think the house became a strange place to everybody. It surely did become strange to me, and my father too became strange to me. From the time he brought Ivy and her boys home with him, I owed everything, simply everything, to Grandmam.

In the old arrangement, my parents had slept in the living room, where the big heating stove stood in the winter. My father slept there still after my mother died, and that was where he and Ivy would sleep. My room was the one above, warmed by hot air rising up from the stove through a register in the floor. Grandmam slept on a cot in the big kitchen at the back of the ell, where she had the warmth, when she needed it, of the cooking stove, and where she kept her rocking chair and her big bureau with its drawers holding her few good clothes and her old clothes and the things she saved because they might be needed.

She had moved herself into the kitchen when my father married my mother. She wanted, as she said, to be out of the way. She wanted my mother to have a free hand with the rest of the house. And in fact she did keep out of the way, and she did give my mother, and then Ivy, a free hand with the rest of the house. Still, by making her last stand in the kitchen, she kept herself in the center of things. In the kitchen she was in charge. Other people who worked in that kitchen worked for *her*. By moving her whole life there, she had, so to speak, faced away from the rest of the house, but from the kitchen she still oversaw the garden, the cellar, the smokehouse, the henhouse, the barn lots and the barns, and all the comings and goings between barns and fields.

She was a good cook, but she also did the main work that kept us eating. She made the garden, and all we didn't eat fresh she preserved and stored for the winter. She took care of the hens and the turkeys. She milked two cows. My father was in charge of the meat hogs, but Grandmam was the authority and head worker at the butchering and sausage making and lard rendering and the curing of the meat. In the summers she, and I with her, roamed the fencerows and woods edges and hollows to pick wild berries for pies and jam. She was always busy. She never backed off from anything because it was hard. She washed and ironed, made soap, sewed and patched and darned. Every Saturday she carried a basket of eggs and a bucket of cream to the store at Shagbark. Though she never made an issue of being the landlady, or needed to, her word on everything having to do with the farm was final. My father understood that, and Ivy didn't change it.

Grandmam was still proud of the narrowness of her waist when she was a young woman. When she married, she said, her waist had been so small that my grandfather could almost encircle it with his two hands. Now, after all her years of bearing and mothering and hard work, she had grown thick and slow, and she remembered her lost suppleness and beauty with affection but without grief. She didn't grieve over herself. Looking me up and down as I began to grow toward womanhood, she would say, "Do you know your old grandmam was like you once?" And she would smile, knowing I didn't know it even though she had told me.

She would do a man's work when she needed to, but she lived and died without ever putting on a pair of pants. She wore dresses. Being a widow, she wore them black. Being a woman of her time, she wore them long. The girls of her day, I think, must have been like well-wrapped gifts, to be opened by their husbands on their wedding night, a complete surprise. "Well! What's this?"

Though times were hard and she was poor, Grandmam was a respectable woman, and she knew she was. When there was a reason for it, she could make herself *look* respectable. But mostly, when she was at home and at work, she wore clothes that many a woman, even then, would have thrown away. Her "everyday" black dresses were faded by the sun and lye soap, and they would be patched and tattery and worn out of shape. For cold weather she had an overcoat that must have been as old as she was, but it was, she said, "still as good as new." In any weather she was apt to be wearing a leftover pair of my grandfather's shoes that were too big. She never gave up on her clothes until they were entirely worn out, and then she ripped them up, saving the buttons, and wore them out as rags.

She was an old-fashioned housewife: determined and skillful and saving and sparing. She worked hard, provided much, bought little, and saved everything that might be of use, buttons and buckles and rags and string and paper sacks from the store. She mended leaky pans, patched clothes, and darned socks. She used the end of a turkey's wing as a broom to sweep around the stove.

She always had one Sunday dress carefully preserved that she wore to church and on her visits to town. For those occasions she had also, during all the years I knew her, a little black hat with a brim and a bouquet of paper violets, which she wore as level on her head as a saucer full of coffee.

My father was not a man of much ambition or, to be honest, much sense about anything beyond his day-to-day life of making do and doing without. It was because of Grandmam's intelligence and knowledge and thrift that we always had a plenty to eat and enough, though sometimes just barely enough, of everything else.

And Grandmam, as I have seen in looking back, was the decider of my fate. She shaped my life, without of course knowing what my life would be. She taught me many things that I was going to need to know, without either of us knowing I would need to know them. She made the connections that made my life, as you will see. If it hadn't been for her, what would my life have been? I don't know. I know it surely would have been different. And it is only by looking back, as an old woman myself, like her a widow and a grandmother, that I can see how much she loved me and can pay her out of my heart the love I owe her.

The day my father went away to marry Ivy, Grandmam lost no time in getting me and all my things moved into the room over the kitchen—furniture, clothes, everything. That room was divided from the upstairs rooms at the front of the house by a hallway and another room that was full of broken furniture and such. When our work was done, Grandmam locked the hall doors and put the keys in her pocket.

She said, "Things are going to be different here, and you don't want to be in the middle of them." I didn't yet know what she meant, but of course she knew Ivy and her boys, and she foresaw what was coming.

By the time my father and his new family got home that night, the change was all accomplished and beyond talking about. As far as Ivy would ever know, I had always slept in the room over the kitchen and those doors had always been locked. Anyhow, we left her free to suppose it.

And so I began, you might say, a new life, and from then until I left home the center of it would be Grandmam.

She took my side. My own mother was gone. Ivy was not going to be a mother to me—as I think Grandmam foreknew, and as Ivy proved. And so Grandmam came back from that distance in time that separates grandmothers from their grandchildren and made herself a mother to me. She disliked Ivy's open partiality to her boys, and so Grandmam made a principled effort to disguise her own partiality to me. And she did usually disguise it pretty well, partly because I felt the need for disguise myself and did all I could to cooperate.

But sometimes Grandmam favored me in ways that she thought were clever and secret but were obvious to everybody and embarrassing to me. For instance, to save sugar we drank our coffee bitter, though with plenty of cream. In fact, I liked it that way. But every so often Grandmam would become unable to bear it—for me, that is, she would just not be able to stand it any longer. I would be sitting with the others at the table, Grandmam standing at the stove, as she preferred to do, to wait on us and then eat her own meal in the quiet later. All of a sudden I would see her hand dart over my shoulder and dump a spoonful of sugar into my coffee. She perfectly believed that she was being too quick and sly to be noticed. But of course everybody saw. I was a grown woman with children before I realized how funny that was, and how recklessly devoted. She was like an old ewe with one lamb.

But her love for me had also more practical outcomes. She said, "You have got to have some money, child."

She was looking ahead. I had not the least idea what she saw, but I understood pretty quick that she was looking ahead. She was thinking of a time when I would not be a girl anymore but would have needs that I would have to meet. Sometimes it seemed dreadful to me that I was coming to a time that would make such demands. But Grandmam was a demanding woman in the present, and she didn't leave me much time to worry about the future.

She had not had much schooling—only eight grades—and so school was a big thing to her. "You have got to learn your books," she said. "You have got to keep at your studies."

And so at night, after the others had cleared out of the kitchen and we had put away the dishes, we would sit down across the table from each other, the best oil lamp between us, she with her work basket and mending and I with my books. We would sometimes look up from our work and talk a little, taking a rest, but neither of us went to bed until my homework was done.

To the extent that she could see to it, I did learn my books. In fact, I became the valedictorian of my graduating class of ten students at the Shagbark School. And again Grandmam embarrassed me by declaring to Ivy and her boys, who were resentful, and to others, who were not the least bit interested, "She is a valedictorian."

As she knew, my need for money was just as serious as my need for book learning. To take care of that, she put me to work, and in that way she gave me knowledge just as worthy as any that I got from books, and of more use. The day we moved me into the room over the kitchen was also the day she told me, "You have got to have some money."

"Listen," she said. "You have got to learn to be some account. From now on, when you're at home and you're not at your studies, I want you to help me."

That was when I was twelve. From then until I was eighteen and graduated from school, I would be at work with her—in the kitchen, in the garden, in the henhouse, in the cowstall. Six years. She was a hard teacher when she needed to be. She made me do my work in the right way. And I learned all the things she knew, which turned out to be all the things I would need to know after I married Nathan in 1948. Though she could not have known it, and she never knew it, the things she taught me were good seeds that sprouted and grew.

She paid me for my work with the surplus eggs and cream that we carried into Shagbark and sold at the store every Saturday. Out of my earnings I bought my clothes and the few things besides that I needed.

That, as Grandmam foresaw, gave me a certain independence from Ivy, who then couldn't blame me for spending my father's money. What I didn't spend, I saved. In the six years I saved $162.37.

Grandmam was an early riser. She got up way before daylight, even in the summer, partly because she had slept her limit, but she took pride in it too, and she gave the habit to me. I would hear her cot creak as she sat up and began to grope her feet into the carpet slippers that she always wore in the house. She would feel her way to the table, strike a match, and light the lamp. She would lay wood in the cooking stove and open the draft. And then, standing close to the heat if it was winter, she would put on her clothes. She would cross the kitchen to the wash table, dip cold water from the bucket, and wash her face. And then she would sit in her rocker to brush her hair and put it up in a bun for the day. As I dressed and made my bed and brushed my own hair, I would listen to her, knowing by the sounds every move she made. By the time I came down the back stairs and crossed the porch to the kitchen, the coffeepot would have begun to whisper on the stove and Grandmam would be cutting out the breakfast biscuits.

We ate while the rest of the household was still asleep, and while we ate we talked. That was our social time. Sometimes Grandmam would tell of her memories of the things that had come to her in her life, many of which by then had been lost, but she spoke of them in her matter-of-fact way, just so I would know. Or we talked of what we had been doing and what we were going to do. She would want to know about school and what my life was like away from her and what I hoped for, and I would tell her while she watched me and listened. She would be studying me. Sometimes I had silly thoughts, and when I told them to her I would know they were silly, she didn't need to say a word. When we had eaten and finished our coffee, we fixed breakfast for the others and went out to milk and do our morning chores.

That was the life Grandmam made for me, and that she used to protect me from Ivy's jealousy and her boys' teasing. It was a good enough life too. After it was over, I realized that it was happier than I had known. We had, you could say, everything but money—Grandmam and I did, anyhow. We had each other and our work, and not much time to think of what we didn't have.

Grandmam saw to it that I worked and learned and saved some money. The time and her character required that. But she also tried to see that I had the pleasures she thought were due me. The "extracurricular activities" at our school were nothing like so numerous as they are now. We had too little money to spare, and all of us children were needed to work at home. But every week we had a ball game that we attended when we could, and parties from time to time, and a sort of May festival at the end of the school year.

When she thought I was old enough, Grandmam allowed me to go on dates with boys. She was strict about the time I was to come home, and the boys would have to present themselves to her before we left and when we got home. She saw to that just by opening the kitchen door and saying, "Young man, come in here and show yourself."

She was afraid I would blunder into an early marriage by getting pregnant or just by being silly. She said, "You're too good and too smart to go to waste. And you're too pretty for your own good, maybe. It could get you an early start on a miserable life."

I didn't mind her watchfulness as much as I might have, and maybe that was because I really was not much tempted by the boys I went out with, though they were good boys and I liked them well enough. I knew that I was a temptation to them, but I had not yet met anybody who even Grandmam would have seen as much of a threat to my future. She had told me exactly what to do if ever anybody got fresh with me. I was to remove their hand firmly from wherever they had put it, look them directly in the eye, and say, "Are you ready to try that in front of Grandmam?" But it was going to be a while before I let things go that far.

3

The Future Shining Before Us

We were the class of 1940. After we graduated that spring and I had made my speech at the commencement exercises about "the future that lies shining before us," I had to start wondering what was going to become of me. Now that I was a high school graduate, I felt that I was a grown woman with a life to live and the future, shining or not, before me. I had an idea of freedom, too. I was wanting to leave home. The bad feeling and the ongoing resentment of Ivy and her boys had begun to be a prison to me. Even my good life with Grandmam seemed not enough to keep me there with the whole world waiting, it seemed like, for me to come out into it. But I was lazy-minded and scared too, and was letting myself just drift along, nowhere near to packing my things and saying, "Well, good-bye. I'm going."

But it wasn't very long before Grandmam saved me any further trouble by making up my mind for me. This was her last gift to me.

One morning when we were finishing our breakfast, she put down her coffee cup and sat looking at me. She did that for maybe a minute, letting me know that she was going to say something important.

And then she said, "Child, dear Hannah, you're grown up now. You have graduated from school. You're a valedictorian. You're smart, and you can do things. This is not the right place for you. You need to go."

My throat ached and I felt tears on my face, for I knew beyond doubt that she was right, and there could be no more waiting. I had to go. And it came to me at the same time, as it never had before, how much she had done for me, and how much I loved her and would miss her.

She looked at me a while again without speaking, dry-eyed, and then she picked up a dish towel and handed it to me to wipe away my tears.

"Listen. Tomorrow morning we're going down to Hargrave. I'm telling you now so you can think about it and get your mind in order. We're going to see what we can do."

My father drove us to Hargrave. Grandmam instructed him to take us to a little grocery store on the main road just where the houses of the town began. He was to leave us there and come back for us at a time Grandmam gave him. She had arranged this, as I didn't yet understand, because she didn't want us to be associated with my father's old car, which looked, as she had often said, like the last of pea time. He of course knew exactly what she was up to, and I remember how he grinned.

When he had let us out in front of the little store, Grandmam waited for him to drive away, and then she turned to me. She said, "We are going to see an old friend of mine."

She looked me over and gave a few improving touches to my dress and hair. I was wearing a navy blue dress with a close-fitting white collar and covered buttons, a very dressy dress, very becoming, that she had given me to graduate in.

She was wearing her good black Sunday dress and her black hat with the violets, her hair neatly done up. As I had never seen her do before, she was wearing too a pair of small silver earrings and a silver broach that matched. To my surprise, seeing her then in the dignity of her best clothes and the strange newness of that day, I saw that my grandmother, as familiar to me as the path to the barn, was a beautiful woman.

Both of us were carrying our purses and wearing gloves.

We didn't have far to go, only two doors to a handsome red brick house in a row of other such houses that stood between the street and the top of the Ohio River bluff. We went across a green lawn with a bird-bath and tall trees, and up the porch steps to a door with leaded glass. Through the glass I could see into a hallway where the light was colored by a stained-glass window at a landing on the stairs.

Grandmam raised the loop of a brass knocker and knocked three times. After a minute we heard steps, and then the door was opened by a white-haired lady, slightly stooped, who looked piercingly at us through her rimless glasses, and then smiled and pushed open the screen door. "Well! Vinnie Steadman! Come in!"

"Hello, Ora Finley," Grandmam said, not ready to come in yet. She stepped aside and reached for me where I was standing behind her. Patting my shoulder with her hand, she stood me where I could be seen. "This is Hannah Steadman." She said it proudly, and then to prove her pride she said, "She is the valedictorian of her school."

I felt myself blush hot to the top of my head, and I had tears in my eyes that I was afraid were going to run over, but they didn't.

"Oh, it's Callie's girl!" Mrs. Finley said in a tone that both sorrowed for my mother and approved of me. She took another of her unhurried straight looks at me and said, "Isn't she fine!" And then, looking back at Grandmam, and with a sort of insistent gesture pushing the screen door wider, she said, "You all come in."

It was a requirement when she said it that time, and we went in.

We followed her into a pleasant living room with a big window looking out to the front, an ornate clock on the mantelpiece, and under the window a radiator fairly loaded with books and magazines. I could hear the clock ticking in a solemn way that made the house seem proper and formal, as Mrs. Finley herself seemed to be. She and Grandmam sat down in armchairs on either side of the big window, and I perched on the edge of a slipcovered sofa on the other side of the room.

Miss Ora—that was what I was going to call her—and Grandmam talked for a while without reference to me. They had been girls together when Miss Ora's father kept the store at Shagbark. They told each other their news or some of it, spoke of the changing times, and named names from the past. There was pleasure and some laughter in all their talk, for they were happy to see each other. And there was something else too, a sort of tone that made you know they were speaking out of the knowledge of age and widowhood and hard times.

After a while Miss Ora said, "And how are Dalton and Ivy and her boys?"

"The same," Grandmam said. "As you would expect."

Seeing Grandmam's reluctance to say more, Miss Ora said, "Hmh!"

and to change the subject looked over at me. She was smiling, but she had sharp, estimating eyes that were not easy to meet, and I blushed again.

"Well, Hannah, you have finished school."

I could only smile back and nod, but Grandmam was quick to answer for me. "Yes. She made A's in all her studies. She was the number one."

Miss Ora said, "Yes. I heard you say that."

"Yes," Grandmam said, talking as if I were perfectly deaf, understanding rightly that I was too shy to take part. "And now she needs to be getting on. She don't need to be any longer at home." She pressed her lips together, looked straight at Miss Ora, and nodded, inviting her to come to her own conclusion.

Miss Ora looked back and then said, "I see."

She had given up talking to me. She said to Grandmam, "And what does she propose to do with herself?"

"She would like to come down here to Hargrave and get a job. There are lots of things she could do. They taught her to typewrite. She can do it fast. And she can write in shorthand. She could work in an office. She could work in one of the warehouses when the market opens. She would catch on. She can do anything."

When I looked at myself in the mirror at home, I saw myself as a grown woman, but out in the world that was asking me to come into it, I was still a girl. I didn't know what to do or what to say. I had no knowledge of my own that would take me past Shagbark. I was inexperienced and unformed—malleable, I think, would be the word. Grandmam knew it. I was a piece of soft clay. I couldn't be that way for long, but while I was she was determined to mold me into something that could stay alive.

It was news to me that I wanted to live in Hargrave and get a job. But hearing Grandmam say so was a relief to me. All of a sudden I could feel myself taking form. I thought, "Yes, that would be all right. Yes, that is what I want to do."

"And she's going to need a room," Grandmam said.

4

Virgil

Dr. Finley had been dead only a little more than a year when I came to live at Miss Ora's. He had been an old-fashioned general practitioner, giving whatever help he could wherever it was needed through the Depression, and taking, I gathered, pretty cheerfully just what he could get of what was owed him. His income gave him and Miss Ora a good life in their good house, but nothing extra. After his death Miss Ora started renting rooms, mostly to tobacco buyers who would be there only during the winter.

So that I wouldn't have to share a bathroom with the men, she rented me her only downstairs bedroom with a little bathroom of its own. It was a snug, pretty room, with a bureau and bed and easy chair, and two big windows looking out across the shady lawn to the house next door. If I angled my line of sight enough, I could see, beyond a beautiful copper beech and a weeping willow, the opening of the river valley. With my few possessions that I brought with me to Hargrave, I had only two keepsakes: a picture of my mother and father not long after they were married, and a beautiful piece of embroidery made by Grandmam's mother. I kept them on the bureau, for they were a consolation. I have them yet.

Miss Ora's house and the two on either side made a sort of neighborhood. There were no fences. Behind the three houses, the backyards mingled into one big garden, with hedges and arbors and lawns and trees and vegetable patches and flower borders that went back to the river bluff. From there you could see the river valley and the big river for a long way up and down. There were fern beds, and gateways with roses trellised over them, and tunnels through the hedges, and a pool with big goldfish, and a gazebo on the brink of the bluff.

This was home to me during the simplest and in some ways the clearest little while of my life. I worked hard while I lived in Hargrave, but after I was settled it was an unworried time. I had never known such prettiness as I found at Miss Ora's. Though she was not by any means a wealthy woman and was busy all the time herself, she had a wisdom that spread order and beauty around her. For me, Miss Ora's was a place of rest. I can remember waking up there early in the morning in that quiet house and hearing the towboats sounding their whistles down in the fog, and a strange feeling of peace would come over me as if from another world.

I had saved enough money to pay my rent and keep me eating for a while, I had enough presentable clothes, and if I ran short of anything I was to write to Grandmam. But I didn't take anything for granted. The morning after I came to Miss Ora's to live, I started looking for work.

I was no good at it. I could work, I knew I could. I had worked at home all my life, and at school I had learned "secretarial skills." As Grandmam had said, I was a good typist, pretty fast, and I knew shorthand. But as soon as I opened my mouth I sounded like I didn't know anything. I was green as a bean and scared, and I sounded like it. There were people looking for jobs who looked and sounded a lot more capable than I did.

I didn't find work very soon, and for a while everything was just odd. I was discouraged and homesick. I missed Grandmam and the old place. I had never been much alone, and in Hargrave I didn't know a soul but Miss Ora.

But knowing Miss Ora was something. For me, in a way, it was everything. Grandmam had known what she was doing when she brought me to Miss Ora.

To start with, Miss Ora knew what it was to be out of place and ignorant and lonely. If she thought I was sad, shut up in my room, she would come and peck twice with one knuckle on my door. "Oh, Hannah," she would say, "don't you want to come out and sit a while on the porch? It's a lovely evening." Or, "Hannah, come back to the kitchen and let's have a cup of coffee. Or tea, if you'd rather."

"All women is brothers," Burley Coulter used to say, and then look at you with a dead sober look as if he didn't know why you thought that was funny. But, as usual, he was telling the truth. Or part of it.

Miss Ora made me come out of my loneliness. She would ask me questions. She would tell me things. She was conscientiously standing in for Grandmam. And the things she told me, as I soon realized, were things she knew I needed to know. She was a reader, and she gave me books to read. She asked my opinion of them and talked to me about them. She didn't approve of everything by "these modern writers," and she talked about the things she didn't approve of. She did this, as I could see, in a way she thought would be helpful to a young lady alone and away from home for the first time in "this modern world."

Before long, when we had got pretty well acquainted, she said, "You must make yourself at home here, Hannah." She meant by that to give me the freedom of the house, as if I were not a renter, though not a daughter either, but maybe a close cousin. I used this freedom to help her any way I could with her work in the house and yard. It was a comfort to do the work, but I liked her too, and I wanted her to like me. I needed her to like me.

And in the ordinary course of things I got to know her family. She had no nearby family of her own, but her sister-in-law was Margaret Feltner, and they were close. Margaret and Mat Feltner lived on a good-sized farm up at Port William. I don't suppose you could say that any of the farmers around here *prospered* during the Depression, but Mr. and Mrs. Feltner had come through it all right—in one piece, you might say. They were quiet, comfortable people. Miss Ora would often have them down to supper, especially when Miss Ora's younger sister, Lizzie, and her husband, Homer Lord, would be visiting from Indianapolis, and they would have a conversational game of rummy after they ate. Or Miss Ora would go up to Port William for two or three days at a time.

The Feltners had a son, Virgil, who farmed with his dad and worked at a warehouse in Hargrave during the tobacco market, and a daughter,

Bess, who was married to Wheeler Catlett. Wheeler was another Port Williamite, born and raised a farmer and a farmer still, but also a lawyer living in Hargrave with an office overlooking the courthouse square.

So I was getting to know some people—some people, it would turn out, who would mean the world to me—but for what seemed to me a long, scary time I wasn't finding any work. I had taken my savings out of the Shagbark bank when I left home and had never opened an account at Hargrave. I was keeping my money in a little tin box, and so I could *see* it dwindling away. I nearly wore out what I had left, counting it, hoping there would be more than I knew there was. I was writing to Grandmam two or three times a week, but since I was keeping my worries to myself I didn't have much to tell her. I was dreading the day I would have to write and ask for money.

Finally it was Wheeler Catlett who saved me. He knew, of course, from Miss Ora that I needed work and what my qualifications were, and so when his secretary, Miss Julia Vye, was taking a little vacation to visit some relatives in Tennessee, he took a chance and hired me to fill in.

When he came to work in the morning, Wheeler was like a drawn bow —lean and tense and entirely aimed at whatever he had to do. Often he would already have seen to things on his farm before he came to the office, and maybe he would be a little late. He would run up the steps, bang open the door, greet whoever was waiting, and sit down at his desk, sometimes forgetting to take off his hat before he went to work.

I would have his mail waiting for him. He would read it and then call me: "Come in, Hannah." I would go in and we would get started on the day's work. He dictated swiftly in strong, clear sentences that he seldom changed.

Busy as he was, he nearly always took time to visit with the old farmers who would be in town on Saturdays and would come by to talk. They were men with long memories who loved farming and whose lives had been given to ideals: good land, good grass, good animals, good crops, good work. Wheeler loved listening to them, and he allowed them to feel that they had a claim on him. One of them was Mr. Jack Beechum, Mat Feltner's uncle, who, later, I would learn to call "Uncle Jack." And there was Mr. Buttermore, who had many political complaints, mainly against the Republicans. I and whoever else was in the outer office would hear him saying loudly, "Wheeler, that damned fellow is so crooked he has to *screw* his socks on."

Also there was Mr. Sterns, a run-down old lawyer with lots of small dealings, who came in one morning, sat down by my desk, and started dictating letters to me. This was a regular happening, but I didn't know it. I took down his letters, being polite, and when he was gone I told Wheeler.

"Oh, type 'em up," Wheeler said, going by. "It's all right."

I had to work hard to keep up with Wheeler, and he was not easy to please. But I knew I had to please him. I needed the work. I needed to make a decent reputation for myself. I went to the office early and stayed late. As soon as I understood him, I saw to it that he didn't have to wait on me for anything.

And I did please him. After Miss Julia came back, Wheeler continued to call me in when he needed extra help. And on his word, as I knew, other lawyers in town began employing me in the same way. Sometimes I would stay with the Catlett children at night when Wheeler and Bess had somewhere to go. I wasn't regularly employed yet, I wasn't what you could call a "success," but my little stock of money in the tin box quit shrinking and began to grow. I started a bank account.

In the fall Miss Julia was sick for a while, and Wheeler asked me to come back. He was busy then, and, looking ahead to tax time when he would be busier, he said, "If you would like to, just stay on through the winter, and then we'll see."

"I would like to," I said.

I had got to know Virgil Feltner when I would see him sometimes on his visits to Miss Ora—"Auntie," he called her. He would stop by on his trips to Hargrave to see how she was, often bringing down a gift of fresh garden stuff or a frying chicken from his parents, and he and Miss Ora would sit and talk.

I liked him right off. He was a rather large man, humorous and generous, always full of Port William news for his old auntie, and very pleasant to me. I thought that if ever I was going to marry, it would be good to marry somebody like him. I thought "like him" because it wasn't possible for me to think that I would ever marry him himself. He was seven years older than I was and far above an uprooted poor girl from Shagbark. So it seemed to me.

In fact, it wasn't possible, then, to think that I was ever going to marry anybody. From the time I first went to work for Wheeler and began to get about in the town a little, I would be asked out on dates. I was asked more often than I went, but sometimes I went. They were passable young fellows, I suppose, my age or just about, but they didn't interest me in the way I seemed to interest them. I would go out with one or another and find that I didn't agree with his opinion that he was the best thing that had ever happened to me. None of them set me aflame with the desire to know him better. One of them I did actually have to ask, "Are you ready to try that in front of Grandmam?" He looked around as if somebody might be watching and said, "Hunh? What?" I can see now that Virgil had placed a mark in my mind that those others couldn't measure up to.

That fall I was working regularly in Wheeler Catlett's office when Virgil began coming down from Port William every day to his winter job at the Golden Leaf Warehouse. I saw him more often after that. He would come in sometimes to see Wheeler on warehouse business, but more often, on the chance that Wheeler might not be too busy, just to visit. Both of them loved farming, and they loved bird hunting and bird dogs. Wheeler was older than Virgil by fifteen years, but, having started out as brothers-in-law, they had become friends.

When Wheeler was busy and Virgil had to wait, he would talk to me. He always came in the late afternoons, and often it would be just the two of us talking together. It made me shy. He seemed to understand this, and he would get me to talk to him by asking me questions. He knew of the old friendship between his auntie and my grandmother. He would ask, "Have you heard anything new from your grandmother?" Or, "What's going on up at Shagbark?" He would listen, and ask more questions, and then fall silent so I would have to ask him, "Well, how are things up at Port William?" and he would tell me. He called me "Miss Hannah."

And then he began bringing me gifts. They weren't much, one rose maybe or the smallest possible box of candy. But they were a lover's gifts. I knew it, and he knew I did. He meant for me to know it. He would present whatever it was with a little bow, pretending to be bashful, making fun of himself and yet honoring me.

He would say, "You know, Miss Hannah, some of these days, when you're older and I'm younger, I'm liable to marry you."

Things got a little complicated for me when Virgil began asking me out. Miss Ora knew about it, of course, and without being exactly blunt, she found ways to let me know it didn't set well with her. She said once, "Virgil sometimes doesn't use all the judgment he's got." And another time: "It's time that boy was getting married, but I don't know who around here would be good enough." She could speak very firmly when she wanted to.

I had to assume she was speaking for the family, though neither of Virgil's parents nor Bess Catlett nor Wheeler ever said such things. I liked them all, and I didn't want to think of myself as a problem to them. Also I pretty much agreed with Miss Ora. I would have had a hard time arguing that I was good enough for Virgil. I had Grandmam behind me, and she had been my foothold. I was proud of her. But I knew too that I also had my poor, unhappy father behind me, and Ivy, and Ivy's boys, and our old farm up there that was looking more tattered and tumbledown every day now that Grandmam was slowing down and Ivy was coming to the fore. And I knew by then that even the wreckage of it was not going to be inherited by me. I could see too that Virgil was in every way a grown man who had found his work and liked it, and was at ease in the world. He was educated. He had been to college. How could I have missed the difference between him and me? I was a half lost, ignorant girl, trying to find my way into womanhood and a decent-paying job.

And so I started refusing Virgil. I would say, "No, I'm sorry. I can't go tonight."

He was courteous. He couldn't easily assume that my reason was any of his business.

But he kept asking. And finally he looked straight at me and said, "Why?"

I wasn't ready for that. Maybe I couldn't have thought of lying to him.

But I didn't stop to think, either. I said, "Because you're my landlady's nephew."

Still looking at me, he smiled and then he grinned and then he laughed. I think he saw it all, but he didn't say so. He said, "Fiddlesticks! Get your coat."

I admit I wanted to go. I wanted to be with him. But for a long time when we went out together it wasn't what anybody would have called a "date." We weren't at first like a courting couple at all. He would take me to supper, or to a movie or one of the traveling shows that used to come around in those days, and then straight home. He was thinking of me as an innocent girl, and he was being considerate, as offish and careful of me as if I were a China doll, or as if Grandmam were watching. He was nice to me, thoughtful and generous in every way, but he never even held my hand. He never gave me the least reason to say, "Are you ready to try that in front of Grandmam?" I knew that he was admirable and I admired him, but I knew too that I had begun to sort of wish he would try something.

Only now and then, in the midst of teasing me or carrying on, he would say, "Miss Hannah, some of these days, when you're grown up, I'm probably going to marry you."

And at Christmas he brought me a present, nothing extravagant even by the standards of those days. It was a slender silver bracelet, the prettiest thing I had ever owned.

Not much changed between us for a long time after that. Except for the way we each felt, which we never spoke about, it was just a friendship. Or it was meant to look like a friendship. For Miss Ora's sake, and so for mine, I could see that Virgil was trying hard to make it look so.

When he came to get me at the house and when he brought me home, always early, he would sit for a while and visit, paying no special attention to me. And he rarely asked me out more than once a week. However convincing he may have been to Miss Ora, he did make things more comfortable for me.

And then, as the days lengthened past the spring equinox and the weather warmed, a change began to take place. Within the old appearance of friendship and Virgil's strict regard for me, something new began to form itself. Often now, instead of going to a show, we would drive in his car through the long evenings, looking at the waking-up country, and often we would stop at some high open place along one of the rivers and look at the country under the moonlight or starlight. And Virgil started talking to me in a different way. He began telling me the things I needed to know in order to know him. He told me what was happening up on his father's place as they were coming to the end of the winter feeding and beginning the spring work. It was better farming by a long way than my own father had ever done. Virgil spoke of how he liked the season and its work, and of what it meant to him. The mule teams were shedding their winter coats and beginning to shine as they left the barn in the early light to begin the day's work. Virgil spoke of that as something old in the world that caused an ancient happiness in him. He was trying to show me the shape of his life, and what might become the shape of it. He was seeing the time to come as a possibility, as a life that he loved. And though maybe neither of us fully understood what he was doing, he made me love it. It wasn't as though I was being swept away by some irresistible emotion. The thought of resistance never entered my mind. When I imagined him entering the life he saw, I imagined myself entering it too. It was becoming a possibility that belonged to us both.

It is entirely clear to me now. We were coming together into the presence of something good that was possible in this world. I have to see it now as a sad hope, because we were able to use up so little of it, but it was no less a beautiful one.

It came to be that when we would sit in one of those lovely, overlooking places, as if we watched a time and a life approaching that in fact was never going to reach us, Virgil would draw me over to him and keep his arm around me as we talked or did not talk. And still he wasn't acting really as my lover. It just seemed that, as we waited together for the coming of this life, it had become wrong to sit apart.

I forget exactly when it was. The trees had leafed out. Warm weather had come. It was early summer, whatever the calendar may have said. We drove up the Ohio a few miles and turned into an old road along an embankment that ended where a bridge had washed out. Below us where we stopped was a low patch of bottomland planted in corn. The little field was nearly surrounded by the trees along the road embankment and the creek and the river.

It was evening, after supper. The sun was already down. We sat without talking in the almost perfect quiet and watched it get dark.

It got dark. The fireflies began to rise up from the ground, shining their little lights. By then you couldn't see what they were rising up from. The darkness over that little field could have been a thousand miles deep. Above us was the darkness and the stars, and below us the darkness of the field and the slow glittering of the fireflies, and the darkness around us.

We were sitting close. And then maybe he forgot himself, or maybe the new being that we together had been becoming moved him past the limit he had set for himself, but in the most lovely, gentle way he did finally lay his open hand on my thigh.

For a minute I didn't have any words at all. And then his name came to me, and I said, "Virgil." And then I said, "Wait. Let's don't and say we did."

He laughed and said, "Let's do and say we didn't."

But he took his hand away, and we sat in the silence again, looking at the flickering lights out in the dark.

And then he said, "Hannah, listen. What if I was to marry you?"

The life we had imagined and wanted seemed close to us. Sitting with Virgil's arm around me, I felt all enclosed in the warm dark and lost to everything that had happened to me so far. Virgil was strong and it made me strengthless. I didn't want to be weak, or strong either. I wanted whatever this was going to lead to. And then I laughed because the place where his hand had been felt cold and I wanted to cry. I said, "If you would I surely would be obliged." I barely had the breath to say it.

He spoke to me then as if I were even younger than I was, as if not sure that I could understand him. "I've been telling you I love you a long time," he said, "in a way you could take as a joke if you wanted to. But I meant it. What you've got to tell me now is if maybe you might love me a little bit. It doesn't have to be a lot right now."

I didn't cry, but I couldn't keep my voice from quivering. I said, "Oh, I do. And not a little bit, either."

I heard myself say that. It gave me a sort of shock, and a cooler, quieter feeling came over me. The things we had said landed me hard all of a sudden on the question of who I was and what I had to offer. I was pretty, and desirable too—how could I not have known that? But I had nothing. I didn't even own a suitcase.

I scooted away from him so I could face him, though I could hardly see him. I said, "I do love you, Virgil. Of course I do. But there are problems with this, you know."

"What?" he said.

And I said, "What will Miss Ora think? What will your parents think? What will Bess and Wheeler think? What will you think in ten years? What are all of you going to think of *me?* You all are prosperous people, with a place in the world, and I don't have anything. Listen! I don't have anything to offer but what's walking around in my clothes."

He started laughing. "That's what I've got in mind," he said. He gave me an actual kiss then, though he laughed all the way through it, and said, "You let *me* worry," and took me home.

I didn't know what he was going to do. What he did was he told his parents at breakfast the next morning, "I'm going to get married."

His mother said, "To Hannah?"

"Yes."

"When?"

"Soon."

He told me that much. What else may have been said, he didn't tell me. Did they object? I would have, I think. When I asked Virgil, he said, "No." He was, after all, twenty-six years old, so maybe they didn't.

Miss Ora, I knew, would have objections, but the others must have thought of that. When I was walking home from work that afternoon, I saw Mr. and Mrs. Feltner in their car backing out of Miss Ora's driveway. They smiled and waved to me and went on.

When I went into the house Miss Ora was standing in the hall, just inside the door. She surprised me. I said, "Oh, hello, Miss Ora!"

She smiled and corrected me. "Auntie," she said, and opened her arms.

———

And so we had the world's permission, you might say, to love each other and to be together. I felt free. I could put my arms around Virgil then and feel that it was rightly done.

When you are old you can look back and see yourself when you were young. It is almost like looking down from Heaven. And you see yourself as a young woman, just a big girl really, half awake to the world. You see yourself happy, holding in your arms a good, decent, gentle, beloved young man with the blood keen in his veins, who before long is going to disappear, just disappear, into a storm of hate and flying metal and fire. And you don't know it.

5

What We Were

Virgil told his parents, "Soon."

But then he told me, "Not *too* soon. Let it soak in a while."

We began to talk, just between ourselves, about what day it would be, but we weren't hurrying.

We were free now, and we saw each other more often. Virgil would quit work early on Wednesday and Saturday afternoons if he could and drive down to Hargrave. We would get something to eat, go to a movie maybe, take one of our drives, stop a while at one of Virgil's pretty places for a little "sloodepooping," as he called it, though he treated me with the strictest honor, according to the old rules. Since by then maybe I couldn't have told him no, it moves me now to remember how careful he was of me. I think it was because he was so much older that he could take responsibility for my youth and greenness and shelter me even from himself. We talked and talked, making plans, foreseeing a life together, and in everything celebrating a delight that was new to me and, I am sure, to him. He had a way of looking at me and laughing, just because he was full of pleasure, and that would make me laugh.

"Oh, I've entirely lost my mind," he said. "I can't remember ever having one." And he hugged me and laughed.

I had the scary duty of taking Virgil to meet my family, not knowing what he would think of them or what they and he would have to say to one another. But Virgil was gracious and respectful to Grandmam, polite to my father, courtly to Ivy, friendly to Elvin and Allen. It went all right.

Maybe it was being there with Virgil that made the old place look poorer to me than ever, and I said as we drove away, "Well, it's not very grand, is it?"

And Virgil said, "Don't think of it. Your grandmother makes it lovely."

The place I associate most with the time of our courtship is that intermingling garden that lay behind Miss Ora's house. If the weather was fine we often walked there. Sometimes we spent whole Sunday afternoons there, wandering about, watching the boats on the river, sitting and talking in the gazebo or on the grass. I would look sometimes at Virgil, knowing that he had been looking at me, and he would be laughing quietly with that pleasure I knew in him, and there would be tears in his eyes.

And gradually I came to know what he had meant when he said, "Let it soak in."

It needed to soak into the family, but it needed to soak into us too, and especially it needed to soak into me.

Like maybe any young woman of that time, I had thought of marriage as promises to be kept until death, as having a house, living together, working together, sleeping together, raising a family. But Virgil's and my marriage was going to have to be more than that. It was going to have to be part of a place already decided for it, and part of a story begun long ago and going on.

The Feltner place had been in that family a long time—since the first white people settled here. Virgil had taken his place, after his father, in the line of those who were gone and those who were to come. It was something I needed to get into my mind. The love he bore to me was his own, but also it was a love that had been borne to him, by people he knew, people I now knew, people he loved. That, I think, was what put tears in his eyes when he looked at me.

He must have wondered if I would love those people too.

Well, as it turned out, I did. And I would know them as he would never know them, for longer than he knew them. I knew them old, in their final years and days. I know them dead.

———

One Sunday afternoon Virgil turned away from the Ohio and we drove up what he called *"our* river." At the top of the Port William hill, he opened a gate and we drove back through the Feltner land to a neat farmstead—barns, a corn crib, lots, sorting pens, a loading chute—with a pair of tall stone chimneys standing down the slope of the ridge not far away. The log house that had stood between the chimneys, fallen to ruin and torn down, was the one where the old Feltners had lived, the first ones.

This was what the living Feltners called "the far place." It was where Virgil kept his cattle. We left the car and walked through two more gates to the chimneys. A shower that morning had cleared the air, and it was a lovely bright afternoon. From what must have been the old front yard, the valley seemed to open almost at our feet. We could see a long way up the river, and downriver nearly to the lock above Hargrave.

Virgil reached toward it with his hand open. "Look."

I said, "Oh, yes! You can see the whole world."

"Almost," he said. "Some of the best of it, anyway."

We stood and looked. The river ran below us, its double row of shore trees swinging in against the hill on our side, leaving a wide bottomland on the other. It needed a long look because you had to think of how old it was, and of how many voices had spoken and hushed again beside it.

And then Virgil took my hand. He said, "It's too good a day not to be here for a while."

We went to the westward chimney and sat in the shade on the old hearthstones. The ghost of the house that had been there surrounded us. All that was left of it were the two chimneys, a pile of the old foundation stones, and the well top with a rusty pump lying beside it.

Virgil said, "They picked a fine place, didn't they?"

"Beautiful," I said.

"God's plenty to look at. Cool and breezy in the summertime."

"Yes," I said, "and cold and drafty in the wintertime."

He grinned and nodded, looking off. He knew I knew what I was talking about.

"The wind lifted the rugs off the floor, I expect. But we've got to build a house somewhere, and we could make it tight."

I said, "Here?"

"It's a possibility, maybe. Maybe we could even use the old hearths and chimneys." He was watching me. "That's just a thought I had. It's a thought you could change. You've changed my thoughts a plenty already."

"Here would be lovely," I said. "Anywhere would be lovely."

He was watching me, still grinning, but he was thinking too. He was serious. "One advantage would be the old well. It's still a good one, I think. They say it was never dry."

He went to the well and lifted away the rocks and boards that covered the opening.

"Come look."

We lay on our stomachs and looked in, blind at first after the sunlight, and then gradually seeing. The well wasn't wide, but it went a long way down. A stone wall went to the bedrock, beautiful as that old work almost always is, and below that the well opened through layer after layer of time to a flat disk of light where we saw our two faces looking back up at us right out of the innards of the world.

As it turned out, that was the last time we ever spoke of building a house there between the two original hearths. War was coming.

We got married in the fall of 1941, after the crops were harvested. We gave our promise of faithfulness until death in a preacher's living room in Hargrave. Bess and Wheeler Catlett stood up with us. There were just the four of us and the preacher and his wife. We made a little wedding trip by train to Chicago, where neither of us had ever been. We felt rather small amidst the noise and gladder than we admitted to be going home when the time came.

Our home—for the time being, as we said—was Virgil's old room at the Feltners'. We had agreed with Mr. and Mrs. Feltner, almost as soon as we had spoken of marriage, that we would live with them until we could build for ourselves. They made us welcome. We weren't crowded, goodness knows. Ten rooms were more than plenty for Mr. and Mrs. Feltner, Virgil and me, and Mrs. Feltner's younger brother, Ernest Finley, who slept in the room over the kitchen, as I had done at home. But once there, we thought no further about building a house. War and rumors of war made a kind of pressure against the future or any talk of plans. And then, after Pearl Harbor, our voices sounded different to us, as voices do in a house after an outside door has blown open.

It was the Christmas season, and we made the most of it. Virgil and I cut a cedar tree that filled a corner of the parlor, reached to the ceiling, and gave its fragrance to the whole room. We hung its branches with ornaments and lights, and wrapped our presents and put them underneath. One evening Virgil called up the Catlett children, pretending to be Santa Claus, and wound them up so that Bess and Wheeler nearly never got them to bed. We cooked for a week—Nettie Banion, the Feltners' cook, and Mrs. Feltner and I. We made cookies and candy, some for ourselves, some to give away. We made a fruit cake, a pecan cake, and a jam cake. Mr. Feltner went to the smokehouse and brought in an old ham, which we boiled and then baked. We made criss-crosses in the fat on top, finished it off with a glaze, and then put one clove exactly in the center of each square. We talked no end, of course, and joked and laughed. And I couldn't help going often to the pantry to look at what we had done and admire it, for these Christmas doings ran far ahead of any I had known before.

Each of us knew that the others were dealing nearly all the time with the thought of the war, but that thought we kept in the secret quiet of our own minds. Maybe we were thinking too of the sky opening over the shepherds who were abiding in the field, keeping watch over their flocks, and the light of Heaven falling over them, and the angel announcing peace. I was thinking of that, and also of the sufferers in the Bethlehem stable, as I never had before. There was an ache that from time to time seemed to fall entirely through me like a misting rain. The war was a bodily presence. It was in all of us, and nobody said a word.

Virgil and I brought Grandmam over from Shagbark on Christmas Eve. She was wearing her Sunday black and her silver earrings and broach. To keep from embarrassing me, as I understood, she had bought a nice winter coat and a little suitcase. She had presents for the Feltners and for Virgil and me in a shopping bag that she refused to let Virgil carry. I had worried that she would feel out of place at the Feltners, but I need not have. Mr. and Mrs. Feltner were at the door to welcome her, and she thanked them with honest pleasure and with grace.

On Christmas morning Nettie Banion's mother-in-law, Aunt Fanny, came up to the house with Nettie to resume for the day her old command of the kitchen. Joe Banion soon followed them under Aunt Fanny's orders to be on hand if needed.

And then the others came. Bess and Wheeler were first. Their boys flew through the front door, leaving it open, waving two new pearl-handled cap pistols apiece, followed by their little sisters with their Christmas dolls, followed by Bess and Wheeler with their arms full of wrapped presents. We all gathered around, smiling and talking and hugging and laughing. The boys were noisy as a crowd until Virgil said, "Now, Andy and Henry, you remember our rule—I get half of what you get, and you get half of what I get." And then they got noisier, Henry offering Virgil one of his pistols, Andy backing up to keep both of his. And then all three of them went to the kitchen to smell the cooking and show their pistols to Nettie and Aunt Fanny.

Hearing the commotion, Ernest Finley came down from his room. Ernest had been wounded in the First World War and walked on crutches. He was a woodworker and a carpenter, a thoughtful, quiet-speaking man who usually worked alone. The Catlett boys loved him because of his work and his tools and his neat shop and the long bedtime stories he told them when they came to visit.

Miss Ora came, still alert to see that I called her "Auntie," with Aunt Lizzie and Uncle Homer Lord, who had come down to Hargrave the day before from Indianapolis. The Lords weren't kin to the Feltners at all, except that Aunt Lizzie and Mrs. Feltner had been best friends when they were girls—which, Aunt Lizzie said, was as close kin as you could get.

And then Virgil and I and the boys with their pistols drove out the Bird's Branch road to Uncle Jack Beechum's place—where he had been "batching it," as he said, since the death of his wife—and brought him to our house. He was the much younger brother of Mr. Feltner's mother, Nancy Beechum Feltner. Mr. Feltner's father, Ben, had been a father and a friend to Uncle Jack, who now was in a way the head of the family, though he never claimed such authority. Everybody looked up to him and loved him and, as sometimes was necessary, put up with him.

Uncle Jack didn't *try* to have dignity, he just had it. A man of great strength in his day, he walked now with a cane, bent a little at the hips but still straight-backed. He was a big man, work-brittle, and there was no foolishness about him.

You would have thought Henry would not have dared to do it, but as we were going from the car to the house he ran in front of Uncle Jack and shot at him with his pistols. I didn't think Uncle Jack would see anything funny in that, but he did. He gave a great snort of delight. He said, "*That* boy'll put the cat in the churn."

And so we all were there.

To get the children calmed down before dinner and so the little girls could have a nap afterwards, we opened the presents right away. The old parlor was crowded with the tree and the people and the presents and the pretty wrapping papers flying about. Nettie Banion and Joe and Aunt Fanny sat in the doorway, waiting to receive the presents everybody had brought for them. The boys sat beside Virgil, who was making a big to-do over their presents, in which he was still claiming half-interest. The boys were a little unsure about this, but they loved his carrying on, and they sat as close to him as they could get.

There were sixteen of us around the long table in the dining room. The table was so beautiful when we came in that it seemed almost a shame not to just stand and look at it. Mrs. Feltner had put on her best tablecloth and her good dishes and silverware that she never used except for company. And on the table at last, after our long preparations, were our ham, our turkey and dressing, and our scalloped oysters under their brown crust. There was a cut glass bowl of cranberry sauce. There were mashed potatoes and gravy, green beans and butter beans, corn pudding, and hot rolls. On the sideboard were our lovely cakes on cake stands and a big pitcher of custard that would be served with whipped cream.

It looked too good to touch, let alone eat, and yet of course we ate. Grandmam sat at Mr. Feltner's right hand at his end of the table, and Uncle Jack sat at Mrs. Feltner's right hand at her end. Virgil and I sat opposite Bess and Wheeler at the center. And the children in their chairs and high chairs were portioned out among the grownups, no two together.

Every meal at the Feltners was good, for Mrs. Feltner and Nettie Banion both were fine cooks, but this one was extra good, and there were many compliments. Of all the compliments Uncle Jack's were the best, though he only increased the compliments of other people. He ate with great hunger and relish, and it was a joy to watch him. When somebody would say, "That is a wonderful ham" or "This dressing is perfect," Uncle Jack would solemnly shake his head and say, "Ay Lord, it is that!" And his words fell upon the table like a blessing.

Beyond that, he said little, and Grandmam too had little to say, but whatever they said was gracious. To have the two of them there, at opposite corners of the table, with their long endurance in their faces, and their present affection and pleasure, was a blessing of another kind.

We were at the table a long time, and while we ate in the dining room, Nettie and Joe and Aunt Fanny ate in the kitchen. When the cakes and custard had been offered again, and everybody had said, "No, no more for me" or "I can't eat another bite" or "I'm already foundered," we were done at last. The men went back to the living room, the boys went to play outdoors, and Bess took the little girls to the quietest bedroom for their naps, while the rest of us women began to clear the table and wash the dishes and set things back to rights. For me, this was maybe the best part of all. We had the quiet then of women working together, making order again after the commotion and hurry of the meal. I have always loved the easy conversation of such times. That day everybody had something to remember, something that others also remembered, about other Christmases and about that day so far, and they told it to enjoy it again and to enjoy it together. When the dishes were all scraped up and stacked, Auntie and Aunt Lizzie and Aunt Fanny and Grandmam sat talking at the kitchen table while Mrs. Feltner and Nettie and I finished up.

When everything was put away and neat again, and all the commotion of the meal seemed a low sound dying away behind us, and Nettie and Aunt Fanny had started home with their presents, we went in and sat with the men in the living room. The talk was easy and quiet there too. Mainly the older ones, out of courtesy to Grandmam, were asking about people they knew in common and testing their memories against one another.

The day wound down. The Catlett girls woke up from their naps. The boys came in chilly from their play and sat in laps until they warmed up again, and then they wandered off. The talk began to have the sound it does when it is coming to an end. Finally Wheeler stood up and said to Bess, "I expect we'd better go." Everybody got up then and began saying good-bye, collecting presents, getting their hats and coats.

Counting noses, Bess missed Andy and went to look for him. She found him finally in the dining room, in the corner at the end of the sideboard, crying. The knowledge of it passed over us all. He didn't know, as we grownups knew, what the war meant and might mean. He had only understood that what we were that day was lovely and could not last.

6

One of the Feltners,
a Member of Port William

And so I became one of the Feltners, and not in name only. I had my place and my work among them. They let me belong to them and to their place, and I needed to belong somewhere. I belonged to Grandmam as I always will, but I didn't any longer belong in her place. Everybody understood that. When Virgil was called to the army in 1942, as we had feared and expected, there was no question but that I would stay on with Mr. and Mrs. Feltner.

I could tell of my sorrow when Virgil went away, but it was not, strictly speaking, *my* sorrow. It was the sorrow of the family, of Port William, of the whole country. A great sorrow and a great fear had come into all the world, and the world was changing. I grew up, it seems to me, in the small old local world of places like Shagbark and Hargrave and Port William in their daily work and dreaming of themselves. I married Virgil in that world, which was his world too though he had been to college. It was the world of our vision of a new house between the old chimneys. It was the world of the Feltners' Christmas dinner in 1941. But then, against the fires and smokes of the war, the new war of the whole world, that old world looked small and lost. We were in the new world made by the new war, into which Virgil and our possible life together had gone away, for a time as I hoped but in fact forever. Our minds were driven out of the old boundaries into the thought of absolute loss, absolute emptiness, in a world that seemed larger even than the sky that held it.

I stayed on in a life that would have been mine and Virgil's but now was only mine. I lived the daily life of Port William that he no longer lived but only read about in our letters.

We all wrote to him, even the Catlett boys. Andy wrote, "Dear Uncle Virgil, I'm restless as a racehorse waiting for you to come home." Like many a young wife of that time, I wrote every day, maybe not a whole letter every day, but at least a part of one, a sort of daily news report from "the home front." As I increased my knowledge of Port William, I had more to write.

The Coulter brothers, Jarrat and Burley, started cropping on the Feltner place during the war, and so I got to know them. I got to know Dorie and Marce Catlett, Wheeler's parents; and Jayber Crow, the barber; and Athey and Della Keith, who had a good farm down in the river bottom and whose daughter, Mattie, was a little younger than I was; and Martin Rowanberry, known as "Mart," who swapped work with the Coulters and hunted with Burley. Jarrat Coulter's two sons, Tom and Nathan, were in the army too, and so was Arthur Rowanberry, "Art," who was Mart's older brother. And so when I wrote to Virgil, I didn't want for something to tell.

I was making myself at home. In the dark way of the world I had come to what would be my life's place, though I could not yet know the life I would live in it. Jarrat Coulter would become my second father-in-law, and Burley would then be my uncle, though I would not so much as lay eyes on Nathan for more than three years. I had come unknowing into what Burley would have called the "membership" of my life. I was becoming a member of Port William.

Port William in fact and mystery, in the light and in the dark—even the name is a stumper. Why in the world would you build a town on top of a hill, or anyhow a ridge, half a mile from the river, and call it a port?

Anybody who lives in Port William is apt to hear that question enough to get used to it. Ben Feltner, Virgil's grandfather, always gave the same answer: "They didn't know where the river was going to run when they built Port William."

He meant, I guess, that Port William has always been, and maybe too that it will always be. I think so. You could say that Port William has never been the same place two minutes together. But I think any way it has ever been it will always be. It is an immortal place. Some day there will be a new heaven and a new earth and a new Port William coming down from heaven, adorned as a bride for her husband, and whoever has known her before will know her then.

Writing about Port William to Virgil in his absence and distance, I realized that the story of even so small a place can never be completely told and can never be finished. It is eternal, always here and now, and going on forever.

I had begun my time of waiting. I was living my life, and yet I seemed somehow to be outside it, as if only when the war was over and Virgil came home would I be able to come back into my life and live again inside it.

And yet I knew I was fortunate beyond anything I might have expected or even dreamed. I had a place unquestionably my own in the world and in Virgil's family. It was a little awkward at first, with Virgil so suddenly gone, and nobody speaking of the fear we had most on our minds. But Mr. and Mrs. Feltner treated me as a daughter of the household, as they had before. And the life of the farm and the household was still undoubted in those days. It went on as it always had and as it needed to do, war or no war, and I did my part. The Feltners were hospitable people in the old way. There was always company, a lot of coming and going, even when we weren't feeding hands. There was plenty of work to be done, lots of housekeeping, lots of cooking and canning and preserving, butter-making, soap-making, washing and ironing, getting ready for company, cleaning up afterwards, looking after the old and the sick, seeing that the grandchildren, when they came visiting, would live to go home again. That was what Mrs. Feltner would say, giggling a little but also meaning it: "I just want them to live to go home."

I loved taking part, I loved being welcomed to take part, but I knew, and the Feltners did too, that I needed to be working and earning on my own. During the tobacco market in the fall and winter I took a job in the office of the Golden Leaf Warehouse, driving down to Hargrave every day with others from Port William who worked at the warehouses in the wintertime. The rest of the year, when I would work part-time for Wheeler Catlett or other office people in Hargrave when they needed me, I would often stay again at the Finley house with Auntie.

Time doesn't stop. Your life doesn't stop and wait until you get ready to start living it. Those years of the war were not a blank, and yet during all that time I was waiting. We all were waiting. This started as soon as Virgil left home, long before he went into the fighting. We all were holding something back inside ourselves that we didn't want to give to that time. None of us ever said, "Oh, if only this war would be over! Oh, if only Virgil can live through it! If only he can stay alive! If only he can make it home!" But we thought those things every day. We thought them and thought them. Each of us knew that the others were thinking them and praying them. And those thoughts made a strange silence among us that we lived around. I, and I think the others too, felt a certain reluctance to have pleasure, as if by waiting for pleasure, by putting it off, by keeping our lives pushed away from us to make enough room for the fear and worry, we might get Virgil safely through the war and home again. And then we would let ourselves live and be pleased entirely.

And yet pleasures came. It was a pleasure-giving house and place, a place we were glad to be. Farming went on, housekeeping went on, cooking went on, eating and sleeping went on, Port William's endless conversation about itself went on. Rationing came, and we joked about it.

Sometimes we would go down to Hargrave and have supper and an evening of rummy with Auntie. Sometimes she would come up to see us. Sometimes, on one of his legal or farming errands, Wheeler would leave Bess with us for an afternoon. She and Mrs. Feltner and I would sit in the living room and talk a long time, quietly, while the clock ticked on the mantel and the sun slowly dropped below the porch roof and shone through the front windows. Sooner or later Bess would say to me, "Well, what have you been reading?" And then she and I would talk about books.

Books were a dependable pleasure. I read more then than I ever was able to read again until now when I am too old to work much and am mostly alone. Back then I read books that Bess and Auntie loaned to me and books from Mr. Feltner's mother's library that was still in her book-cases in the living room. She had been a reader like Bess and Auntie and had bought good books—classics, some of them: Mark Twain's river books and *The Scarlet Letter* and several thick novels by Sir Walter Scott and Dickens. I read *Old Mortality* and thought more than I wanted to of the horrible deeds people have done because they loved God, but it was a good story.

It was a pleasure too when Bess and Wheeler's boys came for long visits in the summertime. They were lively and they carried our thoughts with them out of the house and away from our worry. Or sometimes they took us into worries of another kind. Mrs. Feltner was inclined to foresee the worst.

"Have you seen the boys, Mat?" she would say if Mr. Feltner hap-pened to come to the house.

"Not for an hour or so," he would say. "You reckon we ought to start dragging the river?"

She would laugh at him and at herself. "No. But I do wish they'd stay away from that old quarry."

"And out of the trees and out of the barn loft and off of the roofs," Mr. Feltner would say, and go out again.

Bess, calling up from Hargrave, said, "What are the boys doing, Mother?"

And Mrs. Feltner said, "Going to and fro in the earth, and walking up and down in it."

On warm evenings we would sit out on the front porch from supper until bedtime. There was no TV then, of course, and on weeknights little traffic on the road. It would be so quiet that you could hear other people talking on their front porches or a bunch of children off playing some-where. Besides the night sounds of birds and insects, there would be just the human voices. Sometimes there would be conversation from porch to porch and back and forth across the road.

One August half the town brought chairs and benches to the slope below Mr. Feltner's feed barn where there were no trees, and we sat there late into the night, watching the stars fall.

We were living our lives. We were living the daily history of the households and farms and stores and other work places of Port William. But those lives and that history were kept always ajar by the history of the fighting that came to us day by day as news and sometimes as gossip. Boys, and girls too, were going away into the armed services. Small red-bordered white flags would be hung in the front windows of houses, with a blue star for each son or daughter who was in the service. When the death notices came, the blue stars would be replaced by gold ones. We would hear. Somebody's son would be wounded or killed or lost, and the word from maybe the other side of the world would finally make its way home to some house where it had been so much feared it seemed almost familiar. And then, Port William being Port William, the knowledge would be in every house by the end of the day. You would do the little that could be done: fix some food for the family, pay a visit, say you were sorry, hug the mother or the sister or the widow. Part of the grief would be that the hurt or the dead one would be absent, thousands of miles away. Part of the grief would be that this loss made you somehow guilty, for you were lucky, you were spared, and yet it showed that the worst possibilities were real, for you as for the others.

When Grandmam died in her time in the spring of 1944, and we gave her to her rest at last in the graveyard at Shagbark and heard the beautiful psalm spoken over her, it seemed almost too orderly and natural to be sad.

On Sunday morning and Sunday night and on prayer meeting night, which was Wednesday, we would go to church and receive, it might be, a true blessing of consolation from some passage of Scripture, from one of the good old hymns, or from being together. And we would hear also a sermon in which poor Brother Preston would struggle again with his terrible duty and need to bring comfort to the comfortless, to say something in public that could answer the private fear and grief that were all around him, and he would mostly fail. We would shake his hand at the door as we went out, trying, I suppose, to console him for his wish to help what only could be endured.

One day we knew that Tom Coulter was dead somewhere in Italy. Nothing changed. There was no funeral, no place to send flowers or gather with the neighbors to offer your useless comfort. But this knowledge had come. Jarrat and Burley looked and went about the place as they had before, and yet you knew that great suffering had come to them and they were carrying it in them. The light seemed to fall on us a shade darker. But they had their work to do, we had ours, and we went on.

The time when we didn't quite know what to do was when Virgil came home. That was in August of 1944. Two weeks. It was a time wedged between two absences, a time not so dangerous and a time of danger. Until then he had been on various bases in the states. When he went back, as we knew, he would be sent overseas and into the fighting. It was a time between times, almost a no-time. It was a no-time that led on to a time we could not imagine, and it made us strange to each other. We all were moving in wide circles around our sadness at the coming separation, unable to hide the care we were taking not to speak of what we were thinking.

Virgil was the easiest one of us. He tried hard to make his presence among us seem ordinary, and he succeeded well enough. He kept us talking, made us laugh, helped us to feel that we were doing all right. And yet nothing seemed quite ordinary enough to bring us to rest, not even him. He made visits to people and places, taking me with him, and we talked about everything but the future. He wandered down among the stores and loafing places and talked a while with the talkers and wandered back. He spent a good deal of time out on the place with his dad, working at jobs that mostly he would not see finished. The days were separate and suspended, like plants in hanging pots.

And then on the next-to-last evening we took a picnic, just the two of us, and walked back along the ridges to a place on the farthest one where we could look out over the river valley. It was a place I had never been before.

In a place like that you don't need to say much. For a while we just stood and looked. And then Virgil looked at me and smiled and gave me a little pat.

"I'll build you a house," he said.

I said, "After the war?" I had been afraid to use those words. When I heard myself say them, I was troubled. I hadn't wanted him to hear my longing.

But he was looking steadily at me, and his smile didn't change. He said, "Now too. Now and always. How about here?"

And I said, "Anywhere with you."

There were loose rocks lying around, pieces of old sea bottom, from how long ago? He began picking them up and placing them to mark the corners and doors of a house. As he laid them out, he named the rooms. When he was finished, he brought me in. As the day darkened he set down our basket and I sat down beside it. With dry sticks brought up from the woods, he made a little fire, and we ate our supper beside it.

Of all the kind things he did for me, that house was the kindest. It was a play house, a dream house sure enough, and yet it was the realest thing of all that time. In it we met and were together on the condition only of loving each other. We lived the dearest minutes of our marriage in that dream house, in the real firelight, under the real stars. And when Virgil went away that time I had something of him with me that I would keep.

7

"Missing"

Virgil disappeared sometime after the Battle of the Bulge. We received the notice—"missing in action," with the official regret of the Secretary of War—on March 5, 1945. And what did "missing" mean? That nobody knew where he was? Or where his body was? Or that his body no longer existed, was nowhere, had been blown all into pieces or burnt into smoke that the wind blew away?

It is hard for me to think or speak of the time that came then. I remember it as dark. I can't remember the sun shining, though I'm sure it must have shone part of the time. I would think sometimes with a black sickness of fear and hopelessness and guilt, "What am *I* doing alive?" That was when I was sure that "missing" meant "dead." At other times I would think, "Oh, he has *got* to be alive. They'll find him *somewhere*." And that was a hope almost as fearful as hopelessness.

The pleasures that came then had a way of reminding you that they had been pleasures once upon a time, when it seemed that you had a right to them. Happiness had a way of coming to you and making you sad. You would think, "There seems to have been a time when I deserved such a happiness and needed it, like a day's pay, and now I have no use for it at all." How can you be happy, how can you live, when all the things that make you happy grieve you nearly to death?

A sort of heartbreaking kindness grew then between me and Mr. and Mrs. Feltner. It grew among us all. It was a kindness of doing whatever we could think of that might help or comfort one another. But it was a kindness too of forbearance, of not speaking, of not reminding. And that care of not reminding reminded us, every day, always, of what we felt we could not mention without being overpowered and destroyed. That kindness kept us alive, I think, but it was a hardship too. Sometimes I would have to go to be by myself, in my room or outdoors somewhere, just to get away from it.

Kindness kept us alive. It made us *think* of each other. I could think of myself, of course, with no trouble at all. Justly enough, I could feel sorry for myself. I was a young wife who had been married going on four years, and I had not yet lived a full year with my husband. And now perhaps, possibly, very likely, almost certainly, my husband was dead. Perhaps, possibly, very likely, almost certainly, I was a widow with child by a man now dead, and this child of my love living inside me had become half an orphan before it could be born.

By kindness I was coming to understand what it meant to be in love with Virgil. He and I had been, we were, we *are*—for there is no escape— in love together. I went into love with Virgil, and of course we were not the only ones there. To be in love with Virgil was to be there, in love, with his parents, his family, his place, his baby. When he became lost to our living love in this world, by knowing what it meant to me I couldn't help knowing what it meant to the others. That was our kindness. It saved us, but it was hard to bear.

We knew, always, more than we said. One of us lying awake in the night would know that the others probably were lying awake too, but nobody ever said so. In the daytime it seemed to me that we were all kept standing upright, balanced ever so delicately, by our kind silence. Sometimes it seemed that one word, one outcry, would flatten us all.

The thought that Virgil was dead didn't come upon us suddenly, like "news." It just wore itself deeper and deeper into us day by day.

The difference between me and Mr. and Mrs. Feltner, as I had to see and feel even in my own grief, was that they were old and I was young. I was filled with life, with my life and Virgil's life, with the life of our baby, and with other lives that might, in time, come to me. But the Feltners had begun to be old. Life had quit coming to them, and was going away.

I was young enough for life to be generous with me. The husband I lost in the war, as it turned out, was not to be my only husband. The war that Virgil died in Nathan survived and came home from. But Mr. Feltner lost his only son, his only begotten son. I would watch him go out to his work every day, and I would see that he was going alone, without Virgil who once had gone with him, and I would know that it was going to be that way for him for all the rest of his days.

I would watch Mrs. Feltner when the morning was ending and dinner-time was coming, and she would say what she didn't need to say but always said, "Nettie, put the biscuits in" or "Start the hoecake, Net," and I would know that when two for so long had been expected, now only one would arrive. And this would not change for her either for as long as she would live.

And yet Mr. Feltner would come in smiling. They would greet each other, old lovers, old friends, happy to see each other. He would say hello to Nettie. He would pass some little joke or compliment to me, and I would try to have something to say back. He would go to the sink and wash his hands, and we would sit down to our meal.

Love held us. Kindness held us. We were suffering what we were living by.

I began to know my story then. Like everybody's, it was going to be the story of living in the absence of the dead. What is the thread that holds it all together? Grief, I thought for a while. And grief is there sure enough, just about all the way through. From the time I was a girl I have never been far from it. But grief is not a force and has no power to hold. You only bear it. Love is what carries you, for it is always there, even in the dark, or most in the dark, but shining out at times like gold stitches in a piece of embroidery.

Sometimes too I could see that love is a great room with a lot of doors, where we are invited to knock and come in. Though it contains all the world, the sun, moon, and stars, it is so small as to be also in our hearts. It is in the hearts of those who choose to come in. Some do not come in. Some may stay out forever. Some come in together and leave separately. Some come in and stay, until they die, and after. I was in it a long time with Nathan. I am still in it with him. And what about Virgil? Once, we too went in and were together in that room. And now in my tenderness of remembering it all again, I think I am still there with him too. I am there with all the others, most of them gone but some who are still here, who gave me love and called forth love from me. When I number them over, I am surprised how many there are.

And so I have to say that another of the golden threads is gratitude.

All through that bad time, when Virgil's absence was wearing into us, when "missing" kept renaming itself more and more insistently as "dead" and "lost forever," I was yet grateful. Sometimes I was grateful because I knew I ought to be, sometimes because I wanted to be, and sometimes a sweet thankfulness came to me on its own, like a singing from somewhere out in the dark.

I was grateful because I knew, even in my fear and grief, that my life had been filled with gifts.

Mr. and Mrs. Feltner were a refuge to me. They were a shelter. They just freely gave me whatever they had that they could see I needed. They were always trying to fill the blank that they felt around me. When my pains began on the night of the sixteenth of May, the three of us rode together down to the hospital in Hargrave, Mr. Feltner driving the old car somehow gently, as if the future of the whole world rode in it. They stayed with me through the night, and were there to see the baby almost as soon as she was born. I named her Margaret after Mrs. Feltner, as I thought Virgil would have wanted to do, and as I wanted to do.

When he heard about the baby, my father came. Since Grandmam's death, he had stayed on the old place, farming it now as the tenant of the heirs, namely himself and his brothers and sisters, he being one of six. The times were good for farming then, for a little while, but I knew the farm was running down, for its half a dozen new owners could not agree on much of anything, and would spend almost nothing on upkeep and repairs. Ivy was in charge by then, to the extent that anybody was. As a farmer, my father had declined from his mother's tenant to his wife's hand. And his brothers and sisters, who had five different opinions about everything, were afraid of Ivy and blamed my father for whatever they thought was wrong.

Maybe remembering Grandmam's judgment in such matters, he left his latest old car down in front of Jayber Crow's barber shop and walked up to the house, where he presented himself at the back door. Mrs. Feltner of course welcomed him as she would have welcomed a wise man from the east and brought him to the bedroom where I was lying with the baby and placed a chair for him by the bed.

He was wearing what always passed with him for his Sunday best—a clean pair of bib overalls, a clean work shirt buttoned at the neck, and the jacket of the brown suit he had bought to marry my mother in. He laid his old best felt hat on the floor as carefully as if it had been made of glass. He was fifty-three years old.

Over the years he seemed to have shrunk, trying to make himself invisible to Ivy, or maybe to God. The jacket had begun to look too big for him. I knew he had come in secret. Ivy didn't know where he was.

I told him my news and asked for his. Elvin and Allen were long gone by then, but I asked about them.

They were living up somewhere about Lexington, he said. Ivy didn't hear from them much. He reckoned they were all right.

And how was Ivy?

Ivy was fine. She missed her boys, and was suffering some from the rheumatism, but she was fine.

He too, he said, was fine.

I handed him the baby. "This is Margaret, your granddaughter," I said.

He took her and held her awkwardly and gently on his lap and looked down at her a long time, unable to speak.

Almost from her first day we called her "Little Margaret." She was another gift, surely, to us all. She was a happiness that made me cry. And I was not the only one. I saw, and pretended I didn't see, Mrs. Feltner and Bess and Nettie Banion crying as they rocked her in their arms. We were all thinking, "Poor little child! Where's her daddy?"

Uncle Jack Beechum had left his farm by then and moved into the old hotel in Port William. At the oddest times, and sometimes to Mrs. Feltner's exasperation, he would come to visit me. He would sit by my bed or my chair, watching over me and the baby without exactly looking at us, saying little. He loved me first on Virgil's account, as I knew, but then on my own and the baby's. This was the tenderness of an old man whose love had abided the desire for women for a long time, and had known happiness and hardship and longing and satisfaction and death and grief, and had somehow become innocent again. It was a love almost not of this world, and yet entirely of it. He brought me presents—little sacks of penny candy with their necks twisted shut, or little bouquets from neighbors' flower beds to which he helped himself.

But he himself, though he would not have thought it, was the best present. He had no small talk and few of what are called social graces. He had a kind of courtesy that required few words, and with me a gentleness that was as deliberate and forceful as his bouquets of stolen flowers so roughly broken off. He would say, "Ay Lord, honey, you're all right!" Or: "Here's some flowers I brought you, pretty thing." He knew that I was living in loss, that the baby had been born into loss. He knew, if anybody did, that there was nothing that could be done about it, nothing certainly that he could do, and yet he came. He came to offer himself, to be with us in Virgil's absence, to love us without hope or help, as he had to do. This was a baby that needed to be stood by, and he stood by her.

And he needed her, I think. We all needed her. Even Ernest Finley, an unhappy man, would lean on his crutches and look at her and smile. We didn't know how much we needed her until she came among us, and then we knew. She came to us like love between lovers, the answer to a need we would not have had if she hadn't come.

She was needed, and then there she was among us, growing and changing every day, a living little girl, one of us. At first she was only present, enclosed mostly in her own small being. And then, we could see it happening, she began to look out of her eyes. She began to see the light from the windows. She began to see us. She began to know us. She began to look at us and smile, as if greeting us from a world we did not know or had forgotten. She made sounds at first that were just sounds, and then she made sounds that were answers and sounds that were calls.

To know that I was known by a new living being, who had not existed until she was made in my body by my desire and brought forth into the world by my pain and strength—that changed me. My heart, which seemed to have had only loss and grief in it before, now had joy in it also. I felt myself setting out with that "Little Margaret" into the world and into her life.

She would wake up hungry in the night where she slept in her basket by my bed. I would turn on the light, change her diaper, and then turn the light off. The rest I did in the dark, by feeling. I took her into bed with me and propped myself up with pillows against the headboard to let her nurse. As she nursed and the milk came, she began a little low contented sort of singing. I would feel milk and love flowing from me to her as once it had flowed to me. It emptied me. As the baby fed, I seemed slowly to grow empty of myself, as if in the presence of that long flow of love even grief could not stand. And the next thing I knew I would be waking up to daylight in the room and Little Margaret still sleeping in my arms.

There came a time, long before she could talk, when we knew that she knew her name. There came a time when she began to return our hugs and kisses. There came a time when she began to play, and when Mr. Feltner began to play with her. Mrs. Feltner was a devoted grandmother, but she didn't play. Mr. Feltner was the one who played. When he was in the house and Little Margaret wasn't asleep, he would have her on his lap, teaching her to play patty-cake while she laughed and held to his thumbs. He recited rhymes to her:

> Juber this and Juber that,
> Juber skint a yeller cat.

And he sang to her:

> Old hound dog stole a middlin'
> Many long years ago.

And:

> Did you ever see a spider on the wall,
> A spider on the wall,
> A spider on the wall?
> Did you ever see a spider on the wall,
> A spid—er—on—the—wall?

She could sing that spider song before she could talk.

Soon enough she could talk, and walk, and run, and feed herself after a fashion, and have opinions, and admire her pretty clothes, and make demands. Uncle Jack was careful not to impose himself on her, for fear of offending her, and so she imposed herself on him. She would stand in front of him until he leaned down from his bigness and smiled at her and called her "pretty thing." And she would lift her arms to him.

As if all of a sudden, we couldn't imagine the world without her. She was a part of it, as much as we were, as much as Port William itself was.

Did we spoil her? I can honestly say that I at least didn't spoil her, I was so afraid that she would be a bother to her grandparents and not deserve their love. I sort of knew that she didn't *have* to deserve their love, but I was strict with her. Mrs. Feltner, for one, thought I was too strict, and eventually I saw that she was right.

She said to me one day when I was correcting Little Margaret for something that didn't much matter, "Honey, there are some things it's just better not to see."

Another time, when I had said, "I don't want to spoil her," Mrs. Feltner said, "Oh, Hannah, I always like to see 'em spoiled a *little bit*. It means somebody loves 'em."

Soon enough Little Margaret was three years old, one of us, and Virgil was three years gone.

After we lost Virgil, I grieved for our unknowing love, and for the life we might have lived if we had been allowed to live it. I so much wanted what was lost. It had turned out to be only a hopeless hope, a dream, but I wanted it.

Grieved as I was, half destroyed as I sometimes felt myself to be, I didn't get mad about Virgil's death. Who was there to get mad at? It would be like getting mad at the world, or at God. What made me mad, and still does, were the people who took it on themselves to speak for him after he was dead. I dislike for the dead to be made to agree with whatever some powerful living person wants to say. Was Virgil a hero? In his dying was he willing to die, or glad to sacrifice his life? Is the life and freedom of the living a satisfactory payment to the dead in war for their dying? Would Virgil think so? I have imagined that he would. But I don't know. Who can speak for the dead? Who can speak for the dead whose bodies are never found, who are forever "missing"? Who can speak for a young man gone clean out of the world, whose body was maybe blown all to nothing, in the midst of terrible fear or pain, in the midst of his last prayer?

What I know is this. Virgil loved his life. He loved me. He loved his family. He did not want to die. He wanted to come home and live with me and raise a family, and farm with his dad. He knew we were going to have a baby. He never knew he had a daughter. He never knew her name.

I don't mean to be quarrelsome, but the dead are helpless. I was the mother of a helpless baby, and the wife of a dead man who was just as helpless. The living must protect the dead. Their lives made the meaning of their deaths, and that is the meaning their deaths ought to have. I hated for Virgil's death to be made official. I hated for it to be a government property or a public thing. I felt my grief for him made his death his own. My grief was the last meaning of his life in this world. And so I kept my grief. For a long time I couldn't give it up.

There have been times, then and later too, when I thought I could cry forever. But I haven't done it. There was war and rumors of war. "There was war in Heaven once," as Aunt Fanny would sometimes remind us. But there was something else too.

The living can't quit living because the world has turned terrible and people they love and need are killed. They can't because they don't. The light that shines in darkness and never goes out calls them on into life. It calls them back again into the great room. It calls them into their bodies and into the world, into whatever the world will require. It calls them into work and pleasure, goodness and beauty, and the company of other loved ones. Little Margaret was calling me into life. A little ahead of me in time still, Nathan would be calling me into life.

At first, as the months went by, it was shameful to me when I would realize that without my consent, almost without my knowledge, something had made me happy. And then I learned to think, when those times would come, "Well, go ahead. If you're happy, then *be* happy." No big happiness came to me yet, but little happinesses did come, and they came from ordinary pleasures in ordinary things: the baby, sunlight, breezes, animals and birds, daily work, rest when I was tired, food, strands of fog in the hollows early in the morning, butterflies, flowers. The flowers didn't have to be dahlias and roses either, but just the weeds blooming in the fields, the daisies and the yarrow. I began to trust the world again, not to give me what I wanted, for I saw that it could not be trusted to do that, but to give unforeseen goods and pleasures that I had not thought to want. And so, unknowingly, I was being prepared for Nathan and for my life with him, when that time would come.

Virgil was missing, and nobody ever found him or learned what happened to him. And the girl I was when I fell in love with him and married him began to be missing too, becoming a memory along with him. I was changing, and the world was changing. I was going on into time, where Virgil no longer was. Now, looking back after so many years, I still can recognize that young couple, I know them well, and I pity them for their lost life. But I am no longer one of them. Those lovers fled away a long time ago.

Part 2

8

Nathan

I need to tell about my people in their grief. I don't think grief is something they get over or get away from. In a little community like this it is around us and in us all the time, and we know it. We know that every night, war or no war, there are people lying awake grieving, and every morning there are people waking up to absences that never will be filled. But we shut our mouths and go ahead. How we are is "Fine." There are always a few who will recite their complaints, but the proper answer to "How are you?" is "Fine."

The thing you have most dreaded has happened at last. The worst thing you might have expected has happened, and you didn't expect it. You have grown old and ill, and most of those you have loved are dead or gone away. Even so:

"How're you?"

"Fine. How're you?"

"Fine."

There is always some shame and fear in this, I think, shame for the terrible selfishness and loneliness of grief, and fear of the difference between your grief and anybody else's. But this is a kind of courtesy too and a kind of honesty, an unwillingness to act as if loss and grief and suffering are extraordinary. And there is something else: an honoring of the solitude in which the grief you have to bear will have to be borne. Should you fall on your neighbor's shoulder and weep in the midst of work? Should you go to the store with tears on your face? No. You are fine.

And yet the comfort somehow gets passed around: a few words that are never forgotten, a note in the mail, a look, a touch, a pat, a hug, a kind of waiting with, a kind of standing by, to the end. Once in a while we hear it sung out in a hymn, when every throat seems suddenly widened with love and a common longing:

> *In the sweet by and by,*
> *We shall meet on that beautiful shore.*

We all know what that beautiful shore is. It is Port William with all its loved ones come home alive.

My life with Virgil was a romance, because it never had a chance to become anything else. We were a courting couple, and then we were newlyweds in the shadow of war, and then the war separated us forever. We became only a pretty memory, and now I am the last of its rememberers. Oh, maybe the Catlett boys still remember, but they were too young then to have remembered much. Andy, I hope you do remember, at least a little.

My life with Nathan turned out to be a long life, an actual marriage, with trouble in it. I am not complaining. Troubles came, as they were bound to do, as the promise we made had warned us that they would. I can remember the troubles and speak of them, but not to complain. I am beginning again to speak of my gratitude.

By the time Virgil went into the army, Mr. Feltner and Joe Banion were getting old. Jarrat and Burley Coulter began raising most of Mr. Feltner's crops on the shares, and it was a good thing. He needed their help. He needed their company too. Their losses in the war had made them close, and especially a friendship grew between Mr. Feltner and Burley that was dear and necessary to them.

Jarrat and Burley would often be at work on the Feltner place, and after he was discharged and came home, Nathan would be with them. I was about to say that at first he was nothing to me, but that is not quite right. In Port William, back then, nobody was exactly nothing to anybody. I knew Nathan had been in the war, in the hard fighting in the Pacific at the last. I knew he had lost his brother in the war, and now he had come home to farm with his father and his uncle.

I knew too that the Coulter family had come to a strange pass, having dwindled to a widower and two bachelors, living in two houses on adjoining farms, Burley and Nathan in one and Jarrat alone in the other. Jarrat had lived alone ever since the death of his wife when the boys were young, because that was the way it suited him to live. Burley, according to gossip, had a sweetheart, a might-as-well-be-wife, Kate Helen Branch, and a said-to-be son by her, Danny Branch, but Burley didn't live with them or they with him. What Nathan was doing for company, female or otherwise, I didn't know, and for a long time I didn't wonder. What he was doing was picking up girls at the Rosebud Cafe down at Hargrave, as lonely Port William men have often done. I didn't know it then, and if I had I wouldn't have cared. Well, I don't care yet.

He was not nothing to me, but he didn't matter to me either.

But sometimes my grief for Virgil would become mingled with grief for myself. I didn't want to be selfish. In the midst of so much grief, mine and other people's, I feared the guilt of wanting anything for myself. I had little Margaret to look after and think about and enjoy. Though I had quit working away from home, I was busy every day about the place with Mrs. Feltner and Nettie Banion. So much was a plenty. My conscience told me it was enough and more than enough. And yet time didn't stop, life didn't stop, we learned to believe that "missing" had to mean "dead," month after month separated us from the last we would ever know of Virgil, and in time, against conscience and even will, my grief for him began to include grief for myself. Sometimes I would get the feeling that I was going to waste. It was my life calling me to itself. It was the light that shines in darkness calling me back into time.

That was how Nathan began to matter to me. For a long time after he was home, I looked on him just as a fixture of the life of Port William as it had reshaped itself after the war. But if nobody can ever quite be nothing to you in Port William, then everybody finally has got to be something to you. It took a while. Nathan was a quiet man and not a forward one. To me, he was somebody off on the edge of things, which seemed to content him well enough. But I began to know him. When the men would be working together, I would sometimes carry water to them, or sometimes even dinner if they were working far from the house. Or we would be feeding a harvest crew, and he would be with them. He became a presence to me. It was his presence that gave me the feeling that I was going to waste.

Maybe that was because he seemed so clearly to be going to waste himself. Maybe he wasn't settled at home yet, but it seemed he was just there, just doing whatever he needed to do, which I guessed was the way he had been and done in the army. By then, of course, I knew about the Rosebud girls. One reason nobody could be nothing to you in Port William in those days was that you couldn't help knowing at least something about everybody. I was a little older than Nathan—two years, a long time when you are young—and maybe I felt sort of motherly toward him. He clearly wasn't a settled man or a very happy one. Maybe it didn't occur to me that I was going to waste because *he* thought I was. What *I* thought was, "He needs a woman. He needs a woman of his own. He needs a wife." This seemed merely what anybody would have thought, looking at Nathan as he was then. And in fact, one day when we were finishing up in the kitchen after feeding dinner to the Coulters and some others, Mrs. Feltner said, "I just don't feel like Nathan's as happy as he ought to be. What he needs is a wife."

Nettie Banion said, "Yessum, he does. He needs to buy him some meat and bring it home!"

I could say he gradually assumed a sort of standing in my eyes. He had the hardiness of his father and uncle, their indifference to bad weather, and their sufferance of whatever work or difficulty had come or would come. He was absolutely loyal to them. When they were at work, he was. He was a fine hand. I knew that Mr. Feltner respected him. And young as he was, he clearly had a love of farming that was his own. He was quiet, he never put himself forward, but he was *there*. You couldn't not notice him. And just as slowly as he became a presence to me, I became aware that I was present to him. I knew it by the way he was looking at me.

Nathan was a beautiful man. In my heart and memory he will always be beautiful, but in those days nobody could have missed it. In his quietness and in other ways, he took after his father, but in his looks he resembled Burley. Looking at Nathan, you could imagine how Burley had looked as a young man. He wasn't overly tall, but he was broad-shouldered and strongly made without looking in any way thick. He was as clean cut as a sapling. He wore his clothes and ate and drank in a way that told you he would be offended by anything slovenly.

But his best beauty was in his face, mostly in his eyes. From the time I was first aware of him, I never caught him sneaking a look. He looked at you with a look that was entirely direct, entirely clear. His look said, "Here I am, as I am, like it or not." There was no apology in his look and no plea, but there was purpose. When he began to look at me with purpose, I felt myself beginning to change. It was not a look a woman would want to look back at unless she was ready to take off her clothes. I was aware of that look a long time before I was ready to look back. I knew that when I did I would be a goner. We both would be. We would be given over to a time that would be ours together, and we could not know what it would be.

When I finally did look back at him, it was lovely beyond the telling of this world, and it was almost terrible. After that, we were going into the dark. We understood, and we were scared, and I wanted nothing more than to go into the dark with him.

I was beautiful in those days myself, as I believe I can admit now that it no longer matters. A woman doesn't learn she is beautiful by looking in a mirror, which about any woman is apt to do from time to time, but that is only wishing. She learns it so that she actually knows it from men. The way they look at her makes a sort of glimmer she walks in. That tells her. It changes the way she walks too. But now I was a mother and a widow. It had been a longish while since I had thought of being beautiful, but Nathan's looks were reminding me that I was.

To know that Nathan was thinking such thoughts mattered to me. It mattered to me whether or not I was willing to let it matter, and I wasn't willing. I was unwilling, and I was afraid. In spite of myself, I felt myself changing, but I was afraid to change. I didn't want to be carried away from my old love for Virgil, which I thought my grief preserved, or from my loyalty, which I deeply owed and felt, to him and his family. I was afraid of the unknown, even of my own life that was unfinished and going on.

Nathan began to speak to me, not in a friendly way in passing, in front of company, but as he got or made the chances he began to say things to me that were meant for me alone.

The first thing he ever said in that way was, "Hannah, there's going to be a dance down to Hargrave. I want you to go with me, and I think you ought to let me take you."

Just like that. He wasn't handing me a "line," for sure. It wasn't a request. It was hardly even polite. He had made up his mind and he was telling me, take it or leave it. He wasn't offering me a "date." He was offering me himself, as he was.

I had never called him by name. I said, "I don't think so."

He didn't ask me why. He didn't look or sound regretful. Just a little on the kind side of carelessly, he said, "Well. All right."

He was going to have to make do with the Rosebud girls a while longer, but he had troubled me.

He knew he had. After a time or two, he gave up asking me to go out with him, understanding, I think, the difficulty of that for me. How could I think of going out on dates from the house I had lived in with Virgil, that I still lived in with his parents, the house where Mr. and Mrs. Feltner had so freely made me at home? But after that he continued to talk to me. And I continued to listen, and even sometimes to say something in return. I still looked at him only in glances. It wasn't going to be easy for me to look straight back at that look of his. It would not be easy and it would not be soon. But it became easy to call him Nathan and to listen to him and to answer. I liked him. I had better go ahead and say I loved him, risky as it is to use that word so soon. Your first love for somebody can last, and this one did, but it changes too after promises have been made and time has passed and knowledge has come. But even then, even before the beginning, I loved him. When I felt him looking at me with that look, I felt it like a touch.

It was a strange courtship we had. My love for Virgil had begun in a kind of innocence, leading only in time to knowledge. But what was coming into being between Nathan and me was not a youthful romance. It was a knowing love. Both of us had suffered the war. He had fought in it, and I had waited it out in fear and sorrow at home. We both were losers by it, he of a brother, I of a husband. Now we were coming together out of fear and loss and grief, and we knew it. Each of us knew that the other knew it. That was why Nathan was so direct with me. It was why I kept holding him off. For the time being we were seeing differently, but we were seeing the same thing. We weren't fooling around.

When he would speak to me in our brief encounters in passing, what he was trying to tell me, what he was letting me see though he couldn't tell me, was what he wanted and how much he wanted it. He wanted me. He made that plain enough, and without any roundabout. He was waiting only for my permission, and when I gave it I would know what to expect.

But he wanted more than me. He wanted a life for us to live and a place for us to live it in. I can see it as I saw it then, and I can see it as I know it now. He had gone to the war and lived through it, and he had come home changed. He saw Port William as he never would have seen it if he had never left and had never fought. He came home to these ridges and hillsides and bottomlands and woods and streams that he had known ever since he was born. And this place, more than all the places he had seen in his absence, was what he wanted. It was what he had learned to want in the midst of killing and dying, terror, cruelty, hate, hunger, thirst, blood, and fire.

But this was not a simple desire. In order to have the place, he needed me. In order to have me, he needed the place. He knew these things because he was no longer a simple man. He had come to his desire by going through everything that was opposed to it. Nathan plainly wasn't trying to make it big in the "postwar world." He wasn't *going* anywhere. He had come back home after the war because he wanted to. He was where he wanted to be. As I too was by then, he was a member of Port William. Members of Port William aren't trying to "get someplace." They think they *are* someplace.

Watching him and watching myself in my memory now, I know again what I knew before, but now I know more than that. Now I know what we were trying to stand for, and what I believe we did stand for: the possibility that among the world's wars and sufferings two people could love each other for a long time, until death and beyond, and could make a place for each other that would be a part of their love, as their love for each other would be a way of loving their place. This love would be one of the acts of the greater love that holds and cherishes all the world.

By a long detour through the hell that humans have learned to make, Nathan had come home. He came back to Port William and to me, to the home and household we made, to his family and friends, to our children yet to be born. And of course he came back to loss, to the absence of those who did not come back, and of those who would leave.

There can be places in this world, and in human hearts too, that are opposite to war. There is a kind of life that is opposite to war, so far as this world allows it to be. After he came home, I think Nathan tried to make such a place, and in his unspeaking way to live such a life. Maybe by 1948 I knew already, or I knew before long, that before he went to the army he had been a hunter. After he came home, he gave away his guns. We never had a gun in our house.

In the early spring of 1948, Nathan bought the old Cuthbert place that fronted on the Sand Ripple Road and joined the Feltner place at the back. There were practical reasons for this. Jarrat's farm, which adjoined the Coulter home place, was small, only about seventy-five acres, much of it wooded slopes that weren't farmable. The home place, where Burley lived, was about three times as big, but its future was put into question by Burley's irregular family life and by the existence of his son, Danny Branch, who was then sixteen years old.

So Nathan bought the Cuthbert place, because it was for sale and was what he could afford. That is, he had enough in savings to get the title, a mortgage, and an old rundown farm. He had bought a lot of work. The Cuthbert place had been owned jointly by three generations of Cuthbert heirs who had never been able to agree to sell it but had simply subdivided their interest in it as their numbers increased. There were people in various distant places who every year received one thirty-fourth of half of whatever income the place brought. I had written some of those checks myself when I worked for Wheeler Catlett, who was the executor of the estate. During the war, except for two or three plowlands, the place had been almost abandoned. There were still a few old rock fences on it that were in fair shape. The wire fences were just remnants and patches. Nothing had been repaired or painted for years. Most of the buildings, including the house, were fixable, but whoever was going to fix them was going to have to hurry. There were some wide, well-lying ridges on it, in some places gullied and overgrown, in others not so bad. There were some fine old sugar maples around the house.

Port William had ideas, of course, about what could be done with such a place, and about what Nathan would do with it, and Port William discussed these matters thoroughly, as it always did. It was also mystified:

"Do you reckon he's going to live there by himself?"

"It ain't good for a man to be alone."

"How long do you reckon a family can run on bachelors?"

"Well, Burley ain't exactly a bachelor."

"Well, Nathan ain't exactly Burley, either."

"What do you reckon he's going to do for a woman?"

I knew pretty well what he was *planning* to do for a woman, but it was not easy knowing. In my heart, I wanted to be the woman, but I had a lot to give up before I could be. So did Mr. and Mrs. Feltner.

I knew they were worrying about me. People know more about each other than what they tell each other, and I knew that certain things were obvious. For three years I had led the life almost of an old woman. I had no life beyond the house and the place and the church and the family visits I made with Mr. and Mrs. Feltner. For a long time I didn't need my own life as a young woman. When I began again to feel such a need, fear made it easy to push aside. I feared for myself, and I feared too for Mr. and Mrs. Feltner. Little Margaret was as much a part of their lives as she was of mine. How could I think of parting from them, of putting asunder what had for so long belonged together? I could let my thoughts go to Nathan, but I couldn't think of going to him myself. Mr. and Mrs. Feltner had been parents and friends to me, a refuge in time of trouble. What could I tell them?

One day when Mr. Feltner came in early for dinner, he washed his hands and came on into the living room where I was. I was embroidering a row of flowers across the bodice of a new Sunday dress I had made for Little Margaret. It was close work and I didn't look up. I heard his footsteps. They paused when he came into the room and saw me, and then they came on. He stopped by my chair. He leaned down and laid his hand on my shoulder and made me look up at him. He had tears in his eyes. For a minute we just looked at each other, and then as if in answer to something I had said, or in answer to what he knew I wanted to say, he said, "I know. I know. But, my good girl, you have got to *live*."

He had given me permission. But it was more than that. It was an instruction. It was his wish. I knew he spoke for Mrs. Feltner too. They weren't holding me. They didn't want fear to hold me, for myself or for them. They hadn't known what to do. But now they saw that a life apart from theirs was asking for me. If I wanted it, they wanted me to have it. But they meant more than that. Mr. Feltner was telling me, at his cost, for my sake, what Grandmam had told me eight years before: "You need to go."

And so he raised the dare. If I hadn't cared for Nathan, maybe it wouldn't have mattered. But I did care, and it did matter. The only thing standing now between Nathan and what he wanted was this scared woman looking the other way. To turn to Nathan, to look to him, would be to give my life to the world again. A burnt child shuns the fire. But now I had the feeling that I was expected. I would have to go. I wanted to go. But even sorrow has its pride. Even desire does.

Maybe the world is waiting for you to give yourself to it. Maybe it's only then that things can work themselves out. The next chance Nathan caught, he said, "I want to talk to you."

"Well, start talking," I said.

"Not here."

"Where?"

"Over at the Cuthbert place. Up on the ridge there. Behind the house."

"When?"

"Late this evening. After supper."

"Maybe I will."

Because I needed to walk and to be alone, I often made a quiet wander after supper. I like that time of day. I like to see the country lying still under the changing light and the coming darkness.

It wasn't far, half a mile maybe, back across the ridges toward the opening of the river valley that I could see from the highest ground. At the ramshackle line fence I stepped over from a good farm, well kept for a long time, onto a poor place covered with the marks and signs of neglect. I had to pick my way then, following old grazing paths among young cedar and redbud and locust trees and patches of sumac and black-berry briars. But I knew where the old house was and the ridge behind it, and my winding way took me there. The sun was down. As I walked, the moist evening air bore up around me the good weedy smell of the old pasture.

Nathan was standing among some cedars about as tall as he was. He had heard me coming, or he had known the direction the overgrowth would force me to come from, if I came, for he was facing me. He was standing as quietly as the trees. I was close to him before I saw him, and then I stopped.

It would be a while before either of us moved. But now I was facing him. We were looking straight at each other. I felt a shiver go over me, but I didn't move. I could have cried, but I didn't cry. I had not returned his look before. And now he smiled and nodded, as if to thank me.

And then we looked away from each other. Nathan turned a little and we looked down the slope toward the paintless old house and barns and outbuildings. It was getting dark.

Finally he said, "Well, what would you call this?"

"I guess," I said, "you'd still have to call it a farm."

He said, "It'll never be what it was. It could be better than it is."

We had a little conversation then about the place, what it needed, what could be done, what it offered.

I said, "It, plus what you see in it, plus what you want from it, could be a farm."

He turned and looked at me again. I could hardly see his eyes, but I felt his look.

He said, "It's not the Feltner place," and he meant it as a question. He was asking if I would marry him, and I trembled.

"I wasn't born on the Feltner place," I said. "I was born on such a place as this."

We were looking at each other, though we could barely see. It was almost dark. But to know you love somebody, and to feel his desire falling over you like a warm rain, touching you everywhere, is to have a kind of light. When a woman and a man give themselves to each other, they have a light between them that nobody but them can see. It doesn't shine outward into time. They see only each other and what is between them. If it's only an old run-down, overgrown, disregarded farm they have between them, they see that and they see each other, though everything else is dark.

"I know you're afraid," he said. "And so am I. But can you see a life here?"

I went to him then, and he hugged me. We didn't kiss, not then, not yet. I laid my cheek against him and smelled the smell of his clean shirt and, within it, the smell of him, himself. I put my arms around him then and hugged him as tight as I could. Now that this thing that he had wanted to happen had finally started to happen, maybe he thought I was never going to turn him loose. I wanted to hold and protect and save him forever.

9

Generosity

Nathan and I turned away from the war and saw the future shining before us. The future we faced was no more than the old Cuthbert place, but it shone before us. After all that had happened, I was almost surprised to see that I was still a young woman. I was twenty-six. Nathan was twenty-four. We were young and strong and full of desire. When I looked with Nathan at his place, soon to be ours, we saw it as it was and as it might be. We knew what we would ask of it. We were ready for what it would ask of us.

One big problem remained. It was my problem, and I felt helpless to solve it. Our plans had to be told. If we were going to do what we wanted to do, we were going to have to *say* what we wanted. Port William no doubt already had a good idea what we were up to and was waiting to be told, but the people who needed to be told first were Mr. and Mrs. Feltner.

I couldn't do it. I knew they probably already guessed, but I couldn't see myself telling them. I couldn't imagine the words. For me to tell them, it seemed like, would be to agree somehow to their loss. It would be as if to say that their loss, from now on, would be only theirs, not mine.

I told Nathan, "I can't. I just can't. I'm sorry. What am I going to do? Run away and write them a letter?"

Nathan said, "You don't have to do anything."

That same evening after supper he found Mr. Feltner where he knew to look for him—out on the back porch, smoking a cigar.

"Hello, Nathan," Mr. Feltner said. "Come and sit down."

Nathan stepped up onto the porch and sat beside him. It was a warm summer evening and clear. The light was going to last a long time. Mrs. Feltner and I were in the kitchen with Little Margaret, finishing up after supper. We were making enough noise, and talking away as we usually did when we worked together. We didn't know Nathan was on the place.

Out on the porch, they made the usual comments about the work and the weather.

And then Nathan said, "Mr. Feltner, Hannah and I have been talking. We want to get married. I want to make it right with you."

Mr. Feltner looked at the end of his cigar and thought for the proper words. This wasn't a conversation that went very fast. He said, "It's Hannah's choice, Nathan. It's up to her. I will tell you only what you know. She is a daughter to us."

Then Nathan thought about what he should say, and he said, "I wouldn't ever want her to be any less a daughter to you than she is now, or Little Margaret any less a granddaughter."

Mr. Feltner thought again with his head down, and then he looked at Nathan. He said, "If she loves you, and you love her, you'll be as welcome to us as you can be."

Nathan said no more. To change the subject Mr. Feltner said, "Well, I'm going to gain a better neighbor in this. I reckon you'll keep the line fence fixed." And he laughed. The Cuthbert half of the line fence had been a nuisance to him almost all his life.

"I'll fix the fence," Nathan said.

Mr. Feltner got up and went to the kitchen door and called in, "Ladies, we've got company. Come on out."

Nathan stood up as we came out. Mr. Feltner reached for Mrs. Feltner's hand and smiled at her. He said, "Margaret, Hannah and Nathan are going to get married. Nathan has come to ask for our blessing."

"Oh, bless you!" Mrs. Feltner said, looking at us both, and laughing to keep from crying. "Oh, bless your dear hearts!"

———

And so our tale was told, no longer a secret from anybody. Some in Port William became more interested than before. Some, now that they knew for certain, turned their attention to things they weren't so sure about.

The next day was Sunday. In the afternoon Nathan came and got me, and we went to look at the old house. Until then I had seen it only from a distance. Though he didn't say so, I knew Nathan was worrying. What was I going to think of it? As usual when there was nothing to say, he didn't say anything.

We turned down the Sand Ripple road, after half a mile or so crossed the creek on a board bridge, and after about the same distance again turned into the lane to the Cuthbert place. We re-crossed the creek and followed the lane as it curved around and up the slope to the house.

The house with its shady yard stood in a swag of the slope, well sheltered from the north wind by the ridge behind it, and not far from the walled spring that once had supplied its water. The yard had not been mowed for at least a year. There was no path to the house. The long blades and dead stems of bluegrass lay in mats and tufts under the weeds and several big stalks of burdock. But a patch of day lilies was in bloom along the fence, and an old small-flowered pink rambler rose was blooming in a heap by the gate where we got out of the car.

Nathan unwired the gate. We picked our way across the yard, went up onto the back porch, pushed open the door that maybe never had been locked, and went into the kitchen. The air was musty and hot. The house was full of the stale smell of people long gone and the most complete silence. Going into it was a little like going back to the house of a lonely old widow after her funeral. We felt like we ought to be quiet, and we went quietly into every room. We looked at everything and spoke of what we saw in low voices, as if afraid of being overheard.

It was a house like a lot of houses around Port William: four rooms downstairs, two upstairs, the front rooms downstairs and the rooms above divided by narrow hallways, the rear slant of the roof much longer than the front, the roof in front divided by a gable, a narrow strip of porch along the back, a wider one in front.

In structure the house was tight and sound. It was straight, square, level, and plumb. The rock foundation was solid. The roof would last another ten years. But the marks of hard use and neglect were everywhere. A few useless old sticks of furniture were lying about. The wall-paper sagged or hung in shreds where the winter thaws had sweated it loose. A window was broken. Tribes of wasps and mud daubers had come in to keep house. A pair of wrens were nesting in a gallon bucket on the mantelpiece in the living room. Everything was covered with dirt and dust. There was a dead chimney swift on the kitchen floor. The electric line had come down the creek a few years before, and the house was wired. There was no plumbing. For heat there were fireplaces in the front rooms and stovepipe holes in the chimneys. I would be starting out here at about where I had left off at Grandmam's. Except that here we would have electricity. And this was a better house.

We went into every room and out onto the front porch that had a fine outlook over the narrow little valley of Sand Ripple, and then back through the house and out again onto the back porch. We stood and looked at the old cellar at the end of the porch, the well, the smokehouse and henhouse, the privy leaning like the tower of Pisa out by the garden fence, the two old barns, the corncrib, the buggy shed.

So far, we had spoken only of what we saw. But now Nathan said, "Well, it's fixable, don't you think so?"

I said, "Of course it is. It's a good house. It's our house."

He said, "Here's what I've thought. We'll make it right. We can take all the time we need. We'll go ahead and make at least the downstairs just the way you want it, and then we can get married."

It didn't take me anything like a minute to think about that. I said, "No. Let's go ahead. Let's don't wait."

That was what we did, and I never was the least bit sorry. Nathan was glad too. We didn't care what we would have to put up with, as long as we could be together. "We'll camp in it while we work on it," I said. "We'll tell Little Margaret we're camping out. She'll love that."

We tore and scraped away the loose wallpaper, got rid of the junk and the broken glass, swept and mopped and swept and mopped again. Nathan reglazed the broken sash, and I washed all the windows. We went to Hargrave and bought a new cooking stove and a refrigerator, and that was about the end of our buying for that year. The rest of the household stuff we needed we got out of attics or storerooms at Burley's and Jarrat's and the Feltners'. We furnished three downstairs rooms with what we needed to cook, eat, wash, sleep, and sit down. And then we got married and moved in.

Those were fine days. Everything we did seemed to start something that was going to go on and on. I'll never forget the feeling it gave me just to make this house clean, to fill it with fresh air and the good smell of soapy water, to wash the dingy windows and see the rooms fill with light, to get here one morning and find that Nathan had mowed the yard, sparing the day lilies and the rambler rose. I cut a few blossoms and stuck them in a jar of water in the living room.

From the first day we had all the help we needed, and sometimes more. Whenever the Coulter brothers or the Feltners could spare a little time, some of them or all of them would be over here at our place, doing something that needed to be done. Nathan mended two stalls in the feed barn and brought over a team of mules and a mowing machine. The island of mowed land in the yard soon spread to include the garden, the barn lot, a strip along the lane down to the woods on the creek bluff, and a scrap of pasture behind the barn. Nathan and Burley mended fence for a day or so, and then when they were idle the mules were turned out to graze in the pasture. Before long, a Jersey cow was grazing with them, and her good milk and cream and butter were the first of our own produce that we put on our table. And then Nathan caught a dozen of Burley's half-wild mongrel hens, and we began eating the eggs that Little Margaret and I gathered in our own henhouse.

When we had got ourselves moved in with our hodgepodge of furniture, the house looked bare and spare and incomplete enough. We had no rugs, no window shades or curtains, and the walls were just splotches of bare plaster and old wallpaper. I didn't mind. I had never had a house of my own before, and I was happy. Mrs. Feltner accepted it all in a good spirit, she was even amused by it, but she wasn't as reconciled as I was.

One day she said, "Honey, you have got to have some curtains."

And so she appointed herself and measured the windows and made curtains.

She was right. The curtains civilized the place and gave it a touch of warmth and care that pleased us all.

It was during that time of beginning that I learned really to know Jarrat Coulter, my new father-in-law. It had been no trouble to know Burley, that wondrous, wayward, loyal, funny, grave, thoughtful, tender, solitary, companionable man. Burley had spent a lot of his life alone, fishing, hunting, rambling about in the woods. And he had lived alone after his parents were dead and the boys gone. But he loved company too, and he loved talk. You could get to know Burley in about thirty minutes. Well, maybe that is not quite right. It would be better to say that after you had known him for thirty minutes, you wouldn't be surprised by anything more that you learned about him.

Jarrat was something altogether different. By the time I married Nathan, I had "known" Jarrat for several years, but I still knew him only by his looks and reputation. Looking at him, you knew he was a man who had not spared himself. He had the lean look, not of a young man or of a man at all maybe, but of an old timber after the sapwood has sloughed away. You knew he was either distant or cold or proud or shy, for nothing that he was thinking showed in his face, and he had far less to say than Nathan ever did. By reputation, he was work-brittle and enduring, scornful of hardship and discomfort. People said he had never finished grieving for his young wife. After she died, he had closed up, like a morning-glory in the afternoon. He had learned to live for work, not out of need or greed, and not as a burden, but as a comfort, the mere interest and pleasure of seeing each task accomplished as each year brought it around again.

He was born in 1890. The summer Nathan and I married, Jarrat was fifty-eight, beginning to get old. His hair was white, his eyebrows coarse and gray, his mouth set as if he did not intend to open it until later, and only then for a good reason. But whenever Nathan and Burley were at work at our place, Jarrat would be with them. Sometimes, knowing of something needing to be done, he would come alone. Sometimes when he knew of something that *I* needed to have done, he would come and do it. If there was only one way it could be done, he would just go ahead. If there was more than one way, he would ask me how I wanted it, and he would do it exactly as I asked. Gradually I realized that he was being just awfully kind to me, that he cared about me, that he understood the loss that I had come from to this place, that he wanted me to be glad I was married to his son. And I began the wish, that stayed with me for the rest of his life, to hug him for the sweetness I had learned was in him. I never did, for fear of embarrassing him. Now that I am old, I know I could have done it, it would have been all right, and I'm sorry I didn't.

Little Margaret was in awe of him, and he maybe was a little in awe of her, having had neither a sister nor a daughter. Unless she was in some danger, he seemed never to mind having her in his way, but just smiled and worked around her. They somehow made themselves comfortable with each other without ever saying much of anything. Jarrat had no gab at all. She had plenty, but she would stand beside him and watch him work and never say a word.

Burley she adored, for he never tired of paying attention to her. He would look down at her, make his voice little, and say, "Now, *ain't* she a pretty girl!" As endlessly as she talked to him, he courted, teased, and flattered her. And clowned for her. He could make her cackle.

Little Margaret settled the terms of her friendship with Jarrat and Burley right away. It took her longer to make up her mind about Nathan and our new household. As soon as she knew that I loved Nathan, she held herself away from him and in a funny way kept him under watch. And Nathan, who had not been much with children since he was a child himself, surprised me by knowing how to deal with her. He never offered himself to her until she in some way offered herself to him. He never corrected her until she had made friends with him and he knew she loved him. At first she used no name for him at all. And then she called him "Nathan," as I did. And then, when she realized that her playmates in Port William all had daddies, she began calling him "Daddy."

With the same patience Nathan not only honored his promise to the Feltners that I would remain their daughter and Little Margaret their granddaughter, but he made himself a son to them. He promptly fixed our part of the line fence, as he had told Mr. Feltner he would, and as soon as he could he rebuilt it. As he saw other things that they needed to have done, he did them. He became watchful over them, and gradually they learned to depend on him.

Little Margaret had the freedom of both households, and her trips back and forth were the stitches that joined us all together. She did love all the business of "camping out" with Nathan and me, but she often needed to go back to the Feltners', which for a long time she continued to call "home," and where her room was kept for her just as it had been. We allowed her to go pretty much as she wished, only forbidding her to change her mind after she once had made it up. She couldn't spend the night with her granny and granddaddy and decide to come back to our house, and then decide to go back to the Feltners the same day.

There came a time when Nathan put a gate in the line fence, and a well-worn path went from our house to the Feltners', used first by Little Margaret and then by our two boys, who called the Feltners "Granny and Grandaddy" just as Little Margaret did.

We had made it past hard changes, and all of us were changed, but we were together.

10
Our Place

And so I had put myself in Nathan's hands, mindful also that he had put himself in mine. We were each other's welcomer and each other's guest. And so we had come to our place.

Until we had actually moved in, we continued to call it "the Cuthbert place," as you would call a stranger "Mister." But after we slept there the first night, we called it "our place." And others began calling it "Nathan and Hannah's."

But for a good many years old-timers in Port William, loyal to the past, went on calling it "the Cuthbert place." To anybody looking for us, they would say, "Oh, you'll find them at the old Cuthbert place. Take the first left yonder just past the edge of town, then the first left again after the road has started down the hill. You can't miss it."

If you were bred to the plains or the seashore or the mountains, maybe you wouldn't enjoy it here. But if the Port William neighborhood looks at all like home to you, then you may think this a pleasant place, or even moving and beautiful. It surely is a place like no other. As you start down the hill toward the river, with the woods on both sides of the road, you won't expect it's here. A good many strangers, having been instructed in town that they couldn't miss it, have missed it.

But if you are looking, you'll see our mailbox that still says "N. & H.

Coulter." And you'll see that some of our local "young men" have seen fit to hit it with a big rock so that the door will no longer shut.

Past the mailbox you have left the public behind. The lane dips down, crosses the creek on a bridge that Nathan had rebuilt not long before he died, and then curves gently upward and around the slope in a way I think is lovely. The lane is just a narrow sleeve passing through the trees and the undergrowth. The trees are fairly old, and you know you're passing through one of the orders of the world. And then almost all of a sudden your eyesight widens sweetly out onto the upland, and you see that you've come into an order of another kind, a farm kindly kept, you may say, for a lifetime. You see the house in its shady yard, the barns and other buildings, and the broad, long ridge rising beyond.

What you won't see, but what I see always, is the pattern of our life here that made and kept it as you see it now, all the licks and steps and rounds of work, all the comings and goings, all the days and years. A lifetime's knowledge shimmers on the face of the land in the mind of a person who knows. The history of a place is the mind of an old man or an old woman who knows it, walking over it, and it is never fully handed on to anybody else, but has been mostly lost, generation after generation, going back and back to the first Indians. And now the history of Nathan's and my life here is fading away. When I am gone, it too will be mostly gone.

Sometimes I imagine another young couple, strong and full of desire, coming quietly into this old house that will be empty again of all that is of any use, and will be stale and silent and dingy with dust, and they will see it shining before them as Nathan and I saw it fifty-two years ago. And I say, "Welcome! Love each other. Love this place and use it well. Bless your hearts."

That is the foretelling of my hope. The foretelling of my fear is that no such couple will ever come here again to live in this place and renew it and make their living from it. It could all end in fire, as everybody knows. And maybe the hand of God is in it, who can say? Maybe it won't be a flood and a rainbow this time, but a mushroom cloud and then silence. Which will solve our problems for the time being.

But the cities are overflowing and stepping toward us too. Mr. Feltner used to say in his last years, "You see those old hillsides of mine? Some day they'll be covered up with little huts." Maybe so. Or maybe all our work and care will be bulldozed away to make room for something fancier, for Port William Estates or Sand Ripple Park or Sandhurst or The Meadows.

Most people now are looking for "a better place," which means that a lot of them will end up in a worse one. I think this is what Nathan learned from his time in the army and the war. He saw a lot of places, and he came home. I think he gave up the idea that there is a better place somewhere else. There is no "better place" than this, not in *this* world. And it is by the place we've got, and our love for it and our keeping of it, that this world is joined to Heaven.

I think of Art Rowanberry, another one who went to the war and came home and never willingly left again, and I quote him to myself: "Something better! Everybody's talking about something better. The important thing is to feel good and be proud of what you *got*, don't matter if it ain't nothing but a log pen."

Those thoughts come to me in the night, those thoughts and thoughts of becoming sick or helpless, of the nursing home, of lingering death. I gnaw again the old bones of the fear of what is to come, and grieve with a sisterly grief over Grandmam and Mrs. Feltner and the other old women who have gone before. Finally, as a gift, as a mercy, I remember to pray, "Thy will be done," and then again I am free and can go to sleep.

I am yet well able to look after myself and do my work and see to the place and walk about. In the latter part of the afternoons, after my housework is caught up, and if it is firm underfoot, I take my stick and go out for a walk. Danny Branch and his boys and their boys do all the farming on this place now, as well as on the Feltner place, the Coulter home place where Danny lives, and the Jarrat Coulter place. I go partly to see what they have been doing, and to look at the cattle. Partly I go to see the place.

It is like putting your own foot into your own shoe. Familiar. A comfort. I see the place itself, as it is, and I see all that we have done here, our long passing over the fields that was our living and our life.

It *is* a beautiful place. I go up to the very top of the ridge, and from

there I can look across the Feltner place at the rooftops and treetops of
Port William. Turning the other way, I can see the opening of the river
valley, and across it to the slopes and ridges on the far side. Sometimes
when the evening is fine and there is a pretty sunset, I may stand and
look until the last of the color has left the sky.

Our place, I am proud to say, shows everywhere the signs of careful
use. "It's good-natured land," Wheeler Catlett used to say. "It responds
to good treatment." It responds to bad treatment too, of course, and
quicker, but Wheeler was right. The problem is how to maintain good
treatment beyond an occasional lifetime.

Since we have had it, the place has been laid out in three levels—or,
you might say, in three steepnesses. At the top, on the best-lying or gen-
tlest sloping land, we raised our crops and made our hay. Nathan's rules
from the start were never to plow too much in any year, never to grow
more grain than we needed to feed our own livestock, and never to have
too much livestock. We didn't overgraze the pastures, and we sowed the
cropground to wheat or rye in the fall. So what you see now on these
fields is mostly grass and clover, more than enough in any but the driest
years, and the trees left here and there for shade and of course for prettiness. And there are ponds now in the heads of the draws for stockwater
and fish and for irrigation when we need it.

Where the slopes are steeper and more likely to wash, but not too
steep to mow, we have permanent pastures, and we have tried to keep
the cattle off those places after the ground gets soggy in the wintertime.
A big cow on a soft hillside is a plow, worse than anything except a big
horse. On the steepest ground we have let the woods grow. In some
places the woods is fairly old. In others, just thickets when we came, the
trees by now have grown tall, though of course for trees they are still
young. As trees go, I would say they are getting about old enough to
vote. We have fenced the stock out of the wooded places, first to help the
trees, and then, as we got older, to make it easier to find the cattle.

Sometimes when I go up on the ridge, I walk over onto the Feltner
place. After Mrs. Feltner died, it went to Little Margaret, who at that
time became simply Margaret. She lives in Louisville and doesn't get out
here to see to things often enough, as I'm bound to say. Sometimes she
will come to see me without ever going to see her place. In fact, she

doesn't need to worry, for Danny and his tribe are honest and they are good farmers. But I like to know what is going on, and I go over there to see. The old house is being rented, not to anybody for very long these days, and it is suffering. It has been a long time since I have gone near the house.

Or, if I just want to walk, and especially if I need to be consoled, I go down the lane in front of the house and through the gate and into the woods. What I like about the woods, what is consoling, is that usually nobody is working there, unless you would say that God is. The only trouble with my woods walking is that it is downhill going and uphill coming home.

My path through the woods would hardly show itself to anybody but me, but I use it often enough to keep it followable. It goes around the hillside where it folds into the crease of the steep little stream called Shade Branch. The line between us and the Feltner place follows Shade Branch. The woods is old enough to be fairly free of undergrowth. I go along slowly, watching for whatever may present itself.

Shade Branch, except for a deep hole or two, dries up in the summer. But as the light weakens and the days shorten, the winter rains start it running again. One of the happiest moments of my walks is when I get to where I can hear the branch. The water comes down in a hurry, tossing itself this way and that as it tumbles among the broken pieces of old sea bottom. The stream seems to be talking, saying any number of things as it goes along. Sometimes, at a certain distance, it can sound like several people talking and laughing. But you listen and you realize it is talking absolutely to itself. If our place has a voice, this is it. And it is not talking to you. You can't understand a thing it is saying. You walk up and stand beside it, loving it, and you know it doesn't care whether you love it or not. The stream and the woods don't care if you love them. The place doesn't care if you love it. But for your own sake you had better love it. For the sake of all else you love, you had better love it.

Sometimes Shade Branch gets wild and strong enough to move big rocks. You see what it does, and you know that while the water is running down it is cutting back. It is wearing into the slope, making the hill low, and somewhere exalting a valley. And you know that a day of the world will come when the farm where Nathan and Hannah Coulter made their love and did their work will be gone, not into the hands of another couple or underneath a housing development, but just gone. And you must say, "Blessings on it. Thy will be done."

As Shade Branch comes down near to where it flows into Sand Ripple, about where my path meets it, the descent becomes gentler. You've come to a little patch of bottomland, nearly level, but a rough, unfinished-looking piece of work, even so. The trees like it here and have made a good stand, but there is a lot of undergrowth. The soil is full of the rocks that Shade Branch has gouged out of the hill and carried down and let loose. And everywhere there are old ditches and channels where the stream has run before.

Right at this place is the oldest, biggest sycamore in this part of the country. Hard to tell how long ago, it was struck by lightning that tore off a strip of bark down one side. As it has rotted inwardly it has grown outwardly, leaving a hollow wide enough for a man to lie down in and sleep—which, if the gossip is true, some men have done, and not always alone, either.

One time I asked Burley Coulter, "Do you know that old tree?"

He smiled me one of those smiles of his that could mean anything, and said, "I know it well."

After that, I often thought, "Wouldn't it be wonderful if Danny Branch was begotten inside that old tree?" I reckon there's a fair possibility that he wasn't, but he could have been, and it would have been appropriate.

I do know perfectly that my children made their playhouse in that tree. And sometimes yet when I pass I go inside it and stand a while, and feel enclosed and safe, like a child.

If the water is low in Sand Ripple, you can step across it, rock to rock, just below the old sycamore. On the other side is a strip of bottomland, maybe an acre and a half, tucked in between the creek and the road, that is the most endearing spot on the farm. It is the kind of place that makes you think you'd like to live there if you had another life to live. And it did invite somebody to build a log house there, back long ago when the road from Dawe's Landing to Port William followed the creek—I mean when the road, for a good bit of the way, *was* the creek. Mr. Milo Settle, who used to own the garage in Port William, was born in that house. But the only reminder of it now is a pile of rocks that were the chimney. That is where I go to rest before I begin my slow climb back home again. I sit and let the quiet come to me. It doesn't come right away. I have to quiet myself before I can hear the quiet of the place, and a car passing along the road up on the hillside or an airplane flying over makes it harder. But I listen and wait, and at last it comes. It is an old quiet, only deepened by the sound of the creek, a bird singing, or a barking squirrel. It goes back to the beginning, and in it you can imagine the life of the vanished house.

Over at the foot of the slope, just a little upstream from the house site, you will find the rusted fenders and other parts of a Model T Ford, which is maybe the only remaining relic of the young manhood of Burley Coulter.

This was in the days before Burley's old friend and neighbor Big Ellis had got married. The two of them were leading a free and adventurous life, when they weren't at work. Their freedom and adventure, at that time, depended maybe too much on Big Ellis's old Model T, which he kept going by working on it a lot of the time when he might have been free and adventurous. Sometimes he worked on it with wire and a pair of pliers, and sometimes he worked on it by taking some of it apart and putting it back together. He would quit working on it precisely as soon as it would run again.

One Saturday evening Burley walked over to see if Big Ellis was ready to go. Big Ellis had the car put back together, all except for the steering wheel.

Burley said, "Are you ready? Let's go!"

Big Ellis picked up the steering wheel, clapped it back into place on the end of the steering post, and said, "Let's go!"

He was already shaved and as dressed up as he ever got. He washed the grease off his hands and they got into the car and went.

They went to Port William where they ran into Fraz Berlew, who sold them some moonshine, which he then helped them drink.

When they left Port William by way of the Sand Ripple road, they were in a big hurry. I suppose they had heard of a party or a dance somewhere down by the river. The road wasn't much in those days, and Big

Ellis had the Model T leaping and bounding from one hole or hump to the next.

Burley said, "Can't you slow this thing down? You're fixing to kill us, Big. I ain't worried about you, but I'd hate to see me go."

So Big Ellis slowed it down.

Burley, who never learned to drive, being perfectly satisfied to be wherever he was or wherever he could walk to or wherever he could ride to with somebody else, was a thorough critic of driving and hard to please. He said, "Can't you speed up a little? We'll never get there at this rate."

So Big Ellis speeded up again.

They were going down the hill past our lane. Burley said, "You want to slow down for these curves, Big. I ain't ready to die yet. I'm just a boy."

So Big Ellis slowed down again.

Burley said, "Can't you dodge about half of them rough spots? You're wearing the hide off of me. I won't have ass enough to hold my britches up."

Big Ellis said, "Well, if you know so much about it, why don't you drive?"

And he lifted the steering wheel off and handed it to Burley.

"I steered her to who laid a rail," Burley said, "but she just kept going over the hill."

It went down fast, that slope being in bluegrass then, not trees, and it made, Burley said, "a perfect somersault at the bottom."

"After that," Big Ellis said, "it didn't need to be fixed."

They took the motor out of it to run a hammer mill, and left the rest of it where it still is.

Here, on this place, among its stories remembered and forgotten, Nathan and I made our love for each other. Here we raised our children: Margaret, who came here with us when she was three; Mathew Burley, called Mattie, born in 1950 after I lost our first baby in a miscarriage in 1949; and Caleb, the last, born in 1952. And here is where our love for them was made. Love in this world doesn't come out of thin air. It is not something thought up. Like ourselves, it grows out of the ground. It has a body and a place.

We lived here by our work. Our life and our work were not the same thing maybe, but they were close. The children would grow up knowing how to work, and would have the satisfaction of knowing they were useful. But the foremost reason was we needed their help. From the earliest time they were able to help, we gave them little jobs to do. Sometimes when we expected and required them to do it, work was what they thought it was. Sometimes when we were all at work together, they thought they were playing, but even so work was what it was and they were helping. We were at work, and sometimes hard at work, the year round. By our work we kept and improved our place, and in return for our work the place gave us back our life. The children knew this. For a long time this was the knowledge they most belonged to.

But sometimes too our life in this place was purely our pleasure. Those times would usually be Sundays. Sunday was the day God rested, and except for the chores we too could feel free of work. When the weather was good, and especially on the bright Sundays of spring and fall, we would go on picnics.

Of all the times with the children, those are the ones I love best to remember, when they were still young enough to live free in their imagination. We would make big preparations: food and fishing poles and a can of worms and plans. Would we see Indians? No Indians had been seen lately on Sand Ripple, but who could tell? Wild animals? Oh, we are not likely to see them, but they will see us. Can we build a fort? Oh, yes indeed, plenty of rocks for that. And we'll cook outdoors like the settlers? Exactly. And we're never coming home? Never.

After church we would have a snack to waylay hunger a while, and then we would set out on our journey, the children with whatever plunder they imagined they would need, I with the fishing poles to safeguard the hooks until time to use them, and Nathan carrying our big picnic basket and his axe.

We would wander any of several ways down off the upland, out of the open fields of our workdays and down into the woods, ending up always somewhere in the neighborhood of the mouth of Shade Branch and the old hollow sycamore.

"What about here?" Nathan would say, and he would set the basket down. We would turn the children loose then to run wild in the woods at whatever game or adventure had possessed their minds on the way. I would find a good sitting place with a tree to lean my back against. Nathan would amble about a little as if to get the feel of the place, and then he would take the axe and work up a little wood for a fire. It would be a small fire if the weather was warm, a bigger one if it was cool, but we always had to have a fire.

Nathan had come out of the old time before chainsaws. Like Jarrat and Burley and the Rowanberrys and my father, he was an axman. An axe seemed to fit his hand naturally and almost thoughtlessly. He would look around for dead wood that would split straight and make a lasting coal. When he found what he was looking for, he would make us a neat little woodpile, never wasting a lick. I loved to watch him do that, for it is pretty work when it is done well.

He would build the fire, giving the place a focus and making us at home. We would come to rest beside it. Sometimes Nathan would drop off to sleep. But I was always too busy looking around to get sleepy. In spring, before the leaves were out, the floor of the woods would be sunlit and bright with flowers. In fall, the color would be in the trees, the leaves coming down some days even with no air stirring, brightening the ground, and it would be so quiet you could hear them falling.

The children would get tired of their play and come back, ready to go fishing. Nathan would get up and go with them to see that they didn't hook themselves or drown, and they would fish from hole to hole down Sand Ripple. In the quiet after they left, I would do a sort of housekeeping. The children's make-believe of being pioneers became almost imaginable even to me. In that place of our little journey, as if newly come, I tended the fire and made things neat, unpacked the big basket, spread a tablecloth on the ground, set out the containers of food.

When the fishing expedition came back, I made hoecake and fried up whatever they had caught: sunfish as long as your finger or as big as your hand. If they didn't catch fish, they fell back on crawfish. But something they had caught had to be cooked. And I remember especially how much we belonged together then, how complete we seemed with our fire and our meal, what a unit we were, and the pleasure of it. We ate and talked and rested and played. And then we gathered up our things and walked home again, with just enough daylight left to do the chores.

11
The Membership

Nathan and I had to get used to each other. We had to get used to being two parents to Little Margaret. We had to get our ways and habits into some sort of alignment, making some changes in ourselves that were not always easy. We had to get used to our house. We had to get used to our place. It takes years, maybe it takes longer than a lifetime, to know a place, especially if you are getting to know it as a place to live and work, and you are getting to know it by living and working in it. But we had to begin.

Grover Gibbs was growing the tobacco here that year, and when Nathan bought the place from the Cuthbert heirs, he bought the standing crop from Grover. But we had moved in a long time too late to do much in the way of farming that year. We were too late for a garden, except for a patch of turnips that Nathan sowed in the fall. We were, in fact, camping. But we were making plans too. And we were getting ready.

After the 1948 crop was sold, Nathan bought his first tractor, and so did Jarrat. Burley, who did not know how to drive anything mechanical and did not want to learn, did not buy one.

Burley, at least in the work that he did by himself on his own place, stayed with the old ways, because he saw no reason to change and he was not in a hurry. His son, Danny Branch, who was seventeen that year and had quit school and gone to farming, stayed with the old ways too. This was easier for them both after Danny married Lyda in 1950 and moved in with Burley.

Nathan and Jarrat bought tractors, as nearly everybody else did in the years following the war, because it seemed the right thing to do. A tractor made it possible for one man to cover more ground in a day than he could with a team, and help was scarcer after the war than before. A tractor didn't get tired. With a tractor you could work at night. And so on. But after so much has been said and done, I think Danny has had the right idea. Tractors made farmers dependent on the big companies as they never had been before. And now, looking back, it seems clear that when the tractors came, the people began to go. That is too simply put. But the fact remains that all the Branches are still doing their work mainly with horse and mule teams, and all of them are still farming. And there are a lot of Branches. I, on the other hand, am the last Coulter of the name in Port William.

In 1949, anyhow, we put in our first full year of farming on our place. We started our garden as early as the ground would work and kept it going until the last greens froze down in November. We grew our tobacco again, added a crop of corn, and sowed our first wheat on the croplands in the fall. We got a second milk cow. Through the winter, working at odd times and with whatever help he could get, mostly from Jarrat and Burley and Danny Branch, Nathan had made the old fences stocktight. And in the spring, when the grass had come, we bought our first cattle and sheep. In the fall, after the corn was gathered, we bought our first hogs. As they found time during the summer, Nathan, mowing, and Danny, grubbing ahead of him with an axe, cleared the pastures of weeds and bushes so that the grass began to thrive. Nathan said, "It's beginning to look like somebody lives here."

We didn't have money to do much renovation of anything except the land itself. We had to put the farm to work the first thing. But that year too, we got the barns and other buildings secured on their footings and patched up to the point of usability. We still faced years of work in restoring and improving our place, of doing what we could do for it, of making it capable of doing what it could do for us, but by the end of

1949 we had mostly stopped it from running down, and in some ways it was already getting better.

When Danny and Lyda married and settled in with Burley the next year, that solidified the family work force for the next good many years to come. There were four of us men then, and two women. But in addition to ourselves, a whole company of other people, at different times, in different combinations, might be at work on our place, or we might be at work on theirs. They were Mr. and Mrs. Feltner, Joe and Nettie Banion, Art and Mart Rowanberry, Big Ellis and his wife, Annie May, Elton and Mary Penn, and Andy and Henry Catlett, who in 1950 were just big boys. Of course, we didn't all work together all the time. Sometimes we worked alone. Sometimes Burley alone would team up with Big Ellis or the Rowanberrys. Or Nathan and Elton would work together, or either or both of them with the Rowanberrys. The Catlett boys more often than not would be working for Elton. Mr. Feltner and Joe Banion would go where they were needed.

But there were times too, mainly during the tobacco harvest, when we would all be together. The men would go early to have the benefit of the cool of the morning. The women would finish their housework and then gather, sometimes bringing dishes already cooked, to lay on a big feed at dinnertime; and then, after the dishes were done, they would go out to help in the field or the barn for the rest of the day. Uncle Jack Beechum too would often be on hand to do the little he could, to praise the work of the younger men, and of course to eat with us and pass his compliments over the food.

This was our membership. Burley called it that. He loved to call it that. Andy Catlett, remembering Burley, still calls it that. And I do. This membership had an economic purpose and it had an economic result, but the purpose and the result were a lot more than economic. Joe Banion grew a crop on Mr. Feltner, but also drew a daily wage. The Catlett boys too were working for wages, since they had no crop. The others of us received no pay. The work was freely given in exchange for work freely given. There was no bookkeeping, no accounting, no settling up. What you owed was considered paid when you had done what needed doing. Every account was paid in full by the understanding that when we were needed we would go, and when we had need the others, or enough of them, would come. In the long, anxious work of the tobacco harvest none of us considered that we were finished until everybody was finished. In his old age Burley liked to count up the number of farms he had worked on in his life "and never took a cent of money."

The membership includes the dead. Andy Catlett imagines it going back and back beyond the time when all the names are forgotten. The members, I guess you could say, are born into it, they stay in it by choosing to stay, and they die in it. Or they leave it, as my children have done.

Now nearly all of the membership of 1950 are dead. The still living members are mainly Danny and Lyda Branch and their descendents, the Catletts, who are still here, and me, for the little use I am. There is no longer a Feltner in Port William. The Rowanberrys all are gone. Big Ellis and Annie May were childless. Elton and Mary Penn's children, like mine, have moved away. When I am gone the name of Coulter too will be gone from Port William, most likely forever.

And so an old woman, sitting by the fire, waiting for sleep, makes her reckoning, naming over the names of the dead and the living, which also are the names of her gratitude. What will be remembered, Andy Catlett, when we are gone? What will finally become of this lineage of people who have been members one of another? I don't know. And yet their names and their faces, what they did and said, are not gone, are not "the past," but still are present to me, and I give thanks.

Joe Banion's was the first death. Oftentimes I think of him and of his people, never very numerous in Port William, but here with us from the beginning, members of us, though now entirely gone. Their story here is a sorrow. It was always incomplete, and its ending did not complete it.

Joe died suddenly of a heart attack in 1951. Nettie and Aunt Fanny could have stayed. They would have been welcome, and they knew it. But with Joe gone, they chose to go. They gathered up their belongings and, with Mr. Feltner's and Nathan's help, moved to Cincinnati to be near Nettie's sister, who had moved up there when she married, a long time before. They thought it would be a comfort to be with kinfolks, and maybe there was some charm for them in going north of the great river that had divided slavery from freedom.

I remember the Feltners' grief and my own when Joe died, and again when Nettie and Aunt Fanny went away, and again when Mr. and Mrs. Feltner visited them in their apartment in Cincinnati and found them there but not at home there, and not to be at home again in this world.

If they were going to be at home anywhere it would have had to be in Port William. The Banions belonged to the Feltner place by the same history as the Feltners, going back a hundred and fifty years. The two families belonged to each other. The Banions had been faithful to the place, and their work had gone into it, year after year, generation after generation. The Feltners had been faithful in return, and had favored them beyond the custom. The two families had the same history, they remembered the same things, they knew the same things, there was affection and loyalty between them, and love. And yet the story is incomplete. Its ending was not satisfactory. Nettie and Aunt Fanny had too little to take with them when they left. It was too easy for them to leave. And yet when they left, they were leaving home.

We learned these things by our grief. By our loss too.

My children were born into that story, and into the membership that the story is about, and into the place that was home to the membership, and home to them too as long as they wanted such a home. We brought them up, teaching them as well as we could the things the place would require them to know if they stayed.

And yet, like Nettie and Aunt Fanny, they too chose to go.

12
Burley

When she was about four years old, Little Margaret sincerely believed that when she grew up she was going to marry Burley Coulter. She was not the first young woman to have thought of such a thing.

He would have been in his mid-fifties then and was still an attractive man, as he would continue to be for a long time. If you were a woman and inclined to like him, you would have been more or less in love with him.

Once, after Lyda and Danny Branch had married and come to live with Burley, and he had made them at home with him and himself with them, I asked Lyda, "Have you ever thought what it would have been like to be in love with him when he was young?" And Lyda said, "Oh! Wouldn't *he* have been an armful?"

When he was young, Burley was as wild as you please. He caused a lot of trouble for himself and for other people. He had the gift of construing the trouble into a joke. The joke was almost always on himself, and was a good joke, and so the people who cared about him and were troubled by him almost always forgave him. And so he managed to be wild without being more than temporarily disowned by the family or the neighbors. To use his word, he continued to be a member because they wanted him to be. To use another of his words, he was a wayward member. Later, he was a member because *he* wanted to be.

What changed him, I think, was the death of his sister-in-law. After that, the elder Coulters took Tom and Nathan to raise. A certain responsibility for the boys fell to Burley then. He had not asked for any such responsibility, but he accepted it when it came, and it made him responsible. It made him tender too. He did his part in bringing up his brother's sons, and when his own son, Danny Branch, came along, he did his part for him.

But Burley didn't change completely. He remained always capable of disappearing off into the woods with his hounds, sometimes for days at a time. Until he was old, he could be attracted into what he and his friend Jayber Crow called "celebrations." He didn't think of marrying Danny's mother until too late. All the same, he was good, he was funny, and as much as anybody I ever knew he was interesting.

I would ask him to do something, and he would give me a look that managed to be mocking, respectful, tender, loving, and flirtatious all at once. He would say, "Yes, mam, honey."

Or when a gang of us would be at work in the barn or the stripping room, he would preach the membership, mocking a certain kind of preacher, yet meaning every word he said:

"Oh, yes, brothers and sisters, we are members one of another. The difference, beloved, ain't in who is and who's not, but in who knows it and who don't. Oh, my friends, there ain't no nonmembers, living nor dead nor yet to come. Do you know it? Or do you don't? A man is a member of a woman and a worm. A woman is a member of a man and a mole. Oh, beloved, it's all one piece of work."

"Many hands make light work," Art Rowanberry used to say, and that is right, up to a point. And there is a certain kind of talk that lightens work too. Burley was a master of that. When the work was hard or hot or miserable, or when we were suffering our weariness at the end of a long day, we would hear him singing out: "It's root, hog, or die, boys! I was kicked out of Hell for playing in the ashes! All I want is a good single-line mule and a long row!"

If we were hard at it in the hog killing, he would shout, "Thirty years in a slaughter house and never cut a gut!"

Burley, carrying on. He was faithful, not swift. He would be at the tail end of a crew working across a field, and you would hear him holler, mocking himself, "Follow me, boys! You'll wear diamonds!"

Sometimes as we worked together he would tell stories. That would usually be when there were children around, but all of us would listen.

He told the story of the big picnic that we never had but were always going to have "one of these days."

He told of the time when he was a teamster for Barnum and Bailey's Circus, which he never was, but the idea had caught his fancy, and he made us imagine him driving a team of six spirited black horses with plumes on their headstalls, drawing a wagon loaded with pretty women.

He told of the time he went fishing and the mosquitoes were so big and fierce that he had to take shelter under a lard kettle, and the mosquitoes' beaks were so tough and sharp that they pierced the iron and came through, and he picked up his hammer and clenched their beaks, and the mosquitoes flew off with his kettle.

Jarrat or Nathan always said, "How come you took a lard kettle and a hammer with you when you went fishing?"

And Burley always said, "Some of you fellows don't know *anything*. I been farther around the frying pan looking for the handle, than you ever been away from home."

He told of the night he went to the fair at Hargrave: "I got to feeling pretty good, and I went to this gypsy to get my fortune told. I sat down at her table and shoved her over a quarter. She looked me right straight in the eye and shoved my quarter back. She said, 'I can't tell your fortune. You haven't got anything in your mind.' She was right, too. An honest woman. My head was as empty as a gourd."

He told about going courting one night in a buggy. It was a dark night. It was a weedy place. Backing up to turn around, he backed the buggy onto a sleeping cow, who stood up and turned the buggy over.

Nathan would ask him, "What were you doing courting in a buggy in a pasture?"

And Burley would say, "Now you're wanting to know facts."

He told about the man who bored a hole in the bottom of his boat to let the water out.

He told about the man who woke up dead.

Little Margaret, and the boys when they came along, were always after him for stories. "Uncle Burley, tell us a story. Tell us a story, Uncle Burley." They told "Uncle Burley stories" to each other. The boys both went through times when they wanted to be "just like Uncle Burley" when they grew up.

And so he was the best kind of uncle. The children took a lot of pleasure in him, and maybe for that reason he could require them to take him seriously when he was serious. He could settle them down or talk sense to them or get work out of them sometimes when Nathan and I couldn't. I remember a day when Mattie was about fifteen and we were in the tobacco cutting. We had several loads to unload before we could quit. The day had got long, and it was going to get longer. It was hot and close, threatening rain, and we were trying to hurry. But all of a sudden Mattie dropped down out of the tiers onto the wagon and sat down.

He said, "I've just got to rest a minute. I gave out up there."

He was drenched with sweat, poor old boy, and he had to be tired. But it was the wrong time to quit. Though Nathan was up in the barn where I couldn't see his face, I could hear his silence. I wasn't looking forward to what he was going to say.

But Burley blew a drop of sweat off the end of his nose and gave Mattie a big smile. He said, "You didn't give out. You gave up."

Burley had been handing the tobacco off the wagon. He was about seventy then, was soaked with sweat himself and as tired as the rest of us, but he was smiling. He said, "You might ought to get better acquainted with Old Willie." Old Willie was Burley's name for willpower.

Mattie got up then and climbed back to his place. As time would tell, he was not one for such work, was no kind of farmer, but he never pulled *that* trick again.

Caleb did like to farm and liked to work and was full of enthusiasm. Burley's corrections to him were usually of the opposite kind: "Whoa! Whoa! Slow down there, Lightning! Let your mind catch up with your feet. We ain't got time to quit work and go to a funeral."

Burley could tease them into sense and into work. He could tease them out of sullenness or anger or danger or the dumps. He would make terrible threats against them—"You boys, if you don't stop that, I'm going to climb up on top of you and walk around" or "Boys, I'm about to go to work on you all with a two-handed piss-ellum club"—and they would giggle and do what he told them. It was a kind of wonder. They had no fear of him, they knew better than to take him seriously, and yet they would mind him.

Burley made more or less a secret of being a fiddler, but the family knew it, and a few others. In his younger years he would occasionally take his fiddle to a dance or to someplace where music was being played, as now and again late at night in Jayber Crow's barbershop.

He and Kate Helen, Danny's mother, used to play and sing together. This they handed on to Danny, who could play and sing, and Danny married Lyda, who could sing, and they handed it on to their children. If any of the family were making music, Burley would likely be with them, if he happened to be at the house. He was not always at the house.

As he got old, Burley would sometimes sit up in his room alone and play. Lyda would hear him up there and would tell me about it. He sometimes played fiddle tunes that had belonged to the place in the old times, that maybe he was the last to know, sometimes he played once-popular country songs, and sometimes, though he was not a churchly man, he played hymns. Playing alone, he played slowly. He couldn't finger as nimbly as he used to, but he played slowly, it seemed, just to dwell on the notes. It wasn't the music you would expect, Lyda said, but it was music.

Maybe because of the stiffness of his fingers, he had grown shyer about his playing, but still there would be times when we would go over to sit till bedtime and he would bring his fiddle down and play if the others were playing. His favorite song, I think, was "Wildwood Flower," and sometimes he would ask Lyda to sing it with him. He had sung it once, as a lover, with Kate Helen. Now he sang it with his might-as-well-be daughter, and with the tenderness of his love for her.

One night—this was not long after Mr. Feltner died—toward the end of the evening, he started all alone into "Abide with Me." He played it once, and then looked at Lyda, asking her to sing, and as he started the tune again, she sang. She sang it all the way through, and all of us understood. This was his mourning and his benediction, not just for his friend Mat Feltner, but for Grandpa and Grandma Coulter, Kate Helen, Jarrat, Tom, Uncle Jack, for the membership of his life and ours, its long suffering, past and to come:

Help of the helpless, O abide with me.

All of us were crying by the time they finished. Lyda ceased, and Burley played it through again, a final time, slowly, leaning forward as if the better to pour the music out of the f-holes. He laid the fiddle across his lap, wiped his tears on the back of his hand, looked at us and smiled, and then he laughed his laugh of pleasure at what they had done.

13
Ivy

I have not been back to our old place, Grandmam's place, at Shagbark since my father died. It is dear to me, or the memory of it is, but for a long time I feared the sight of what had become of it.

After Elvin and Allen were gone and my father was dead, Ivy lived on alone in the old house for a while. But the house was getting ready to tumble down on top of Ivy, who by then was living in the kitchen, and there was no longer any reason for the family to "hang on to it," as they said. And so the place was bought as "an investment" by some people in Cincinnati, who promptly solved the problem of the old house by burning it down and replacing it with a mobile home.

This was no proper concern of mine, since Ivy, as Grandmam had foreseen, was my father's only heir. From her his inheritance, if anything was left of it, was to pass to Elvin and Allen. But without trying to know, I knew everything that happened, for of course there are always people who volunteer to keep you informed.

With her share of the proceeds from the sale of the place and her checks from Social Security, Ivy made her last stand in a used mobile home of her own on the site of another burnt house next to the store, now shut, at Shagbark.

I would tell myself that Ivy's fate was not my concern. But of course it was, for I had never ceased to think of her. The hardest resentments to give up are the ones you felt knowingly as a child, and I had kept a list of resentments against Ivy. I never reconciled myself to her marriage to my father, which I continued to think had damaged him and insulted my mother. And I remembered every one of her injustices to me. I had hated her for her power over us, and at times I had been afraid of her. I had enough imagination to know what a life I would have lived if it had not been for Grandmam.

After Grandmam died, I imagined that my father would give me her silver broach and earrings. I used too much imagination that time, for he did not give them to me, and I knew perfectly that Ivy had taken them for herself.

I don't want you to think, Andy Catlett, that I dwelt on the subject of Ivy. I didn't. I had a plenty else to think about. I was a grown woman with a husband and children and a place of my own. I had a good life, and I knew it. But I was not forgetting Ivy, either. From time to time, too often maybe, I thought of her, and when I thought of her I thought of the broach and earrings that she did not deserve and was unworthy to wear. That thought, when I had it on my mind, was like a grain of corn in my shoe.

And then one afternoon, when the thought of Ivy was miles away, I met her.

I had gone into the dry goods store at Hargrave, the old Klinger's Dry Goods that by now stands as empty as the store at Shagbark, to look for dress material. Mrs. Klinger was showing me what they had while I looked and felt and mused. And then I was aware that an old woman whose head hardly came to my shoulder was standing beside me.

She was wearing a head scarf and a dress that hung on her as it would have hung on a chair. She was shrunken and twisted by arthritis and was leaning on two canes. Her hands were so knotted as hardly to look like hands. She was smiling at me. She said, "You don't know me, do you?"

I knew her then, and almost instantly there were tears on my face. I started feeling in my purse for a handkerchief and tried to be able to say something. All kinds of knowledge came to me, all in a sort of flare in my mind. I knew for one thing that she was more simpleminded than I had ever thought. She had perfectly forgot, or had never known, how much and how justly I had resented her. But I knew at the same instant that my resentment was gone, just gone. And the fear of her that was once so big in me, where was it? And who was this poor sufferer who stood there with me?

"Yes, Ivy, I know you," I said, and I sounded kind.

I didn't understand exactly what had happened until the thought of her woke me up in the middle of that night, and I was saying to myself, "You have *forgiven* her."

I had. My old hatred and contempt and fear, that I had kept so carefully so long, were gone, and I was free.

14

The Room of Love

I was twenty-six years getting from my birth in the old house on the Steadman place at Shagbark to a house and place of my own, and to a long-going, day-to-day marriage. As I said before, the marriage had troubles in it, which is easy to say. It had something else in it too, which is not so easy. As I go about quietly by myself in my days now or lie awake in the night, I hunt for the way to speak of it, for it is the best thing I have known in this world, and it lays its peace on everything else I know.

What the marriage had in it, of course, was Nathan and me. We were in it together because of our plighting of troth, his to me, mine to him, and that was one thing. But we were together in it also because, from time to time, often enough, we were in it by desire, we met entirely in it and were one flesh. What that was and is and means is not altogether going to be found in words.

This was a marriage that did not begin with a honeymoon, and that tells one of the important things about it. We got married and went to work. We had to, we didn't have time or money to spare. And a honeymoon was something we never greatly missed. Nathan said, "It would have been nice if we'd had it, but we didn't have it." We had our living to make, and our place to make while we made our living. We were at work pretty quick after the groom kissed the bride. We had debts to pay and a long effort ahead of us.

The making of the place was the thing that ruled over everything else, for we were living from the place. Little Margaret, and our boys after they came, were living from the place. You can see that it is hard to mark the difference between our life and our place, our place and ourselves.

As the years passed and our life changed, the place changed. It emerged, you might say, from what it had been into what we needed and wanted it to be, never perfect of course, but always a little better. It came under the influence of what we foresaw in it, and of our ways of using it and going about in it.

Though we talked of what was possible and what needed to be done, the shaping of the place, the look of it, was mostly Nathan's doing. He had a way of getting it right.

He didn't want to come out and say so, but he was proud of his work.

When Andy Catlett would come back after one of his longish absences from home and would come to see us, Nathan would ask him, "Well, do you see anything different?"

It would be a new building or an old one renewed or a new fence, or a coat of paint somewhere. Andy would shake his head and grin, knowing he was being tested and was failing the test. Nathan would have to tell him, "Look at the barn" or "Look at the lot fence" or "Look at the corncrib."

Andy would say, "Oh!" and make the proper compliment, for he would be honestly pleased as soon as he saw what he needed to see.

Later Nathan would laugh. "He's the same damned dreamy kid he's always been."

But this wasn't exactly Andy's fault. What Nathan had done was what should have been done. The place never looked as if something had been changed. It looked right. It looked the way it ought to have looked. It looked right because the right man was doing the work. If the wrong man had done it, Andy, even you would have noticed.

Nathan always got up before I did. If it was winter he would build the fires. As the children grew big enough to have their own morning chores, he would get them up. I would hear them go out. The nighttime quiet would fill the house again. And then I would get up and dress and go to the kitchen. I would have breakfast ready by the time they came in with the milk.

Except when I was needed in the crew work of the busiest farming seasons, I kept the house, worked in the garden, and took care of the chickens, doing the work again that I had done with Grandmam when I was a girl, except that now I usually didn't do the milking. As I went about my work then as a young woman, and still now when I am old, Grandmam has been often close to me in my thoughts. And again I come to the difficulty of finding words. It is hard to say what it means to be at work and thinking of a person you loved and love still who did that same work before you and who taught you to do it. It is a comfort ever and always, like hearing the rhyme come when you are singing a song.

The house, its furnishings and surroundings, took on the appearance given it by my ways of work and my liking, just as Nathan's work and his liking altered the looks of the farm. And as our work shaped our workplaces, our work and our workplaces shaped our days. Our work brought us together and drew us apart. Sometimes we would be together only at mealtimes and at night. Sometimes we would be together at the same work most of the day.

We had differences. There were the agreed-on differences of work. There were the accepted, mostly happy differences between a man and a woman. There were the differences of nature and character that were sometimes happy and sometimes not. Some of the things that most endeared Nathan to me—his quietness, his love of his work, his determination—were the things that could sometimes make me maddest at him.

He hated waste, and he was not a waster. It is not surprising that he did not waste words. He said exactly what he had to say, and he meant what he said. He was inclined not to say again what he had said before. You had to listen to him, as the children knew, because he wasn't going to repeat himself. Sometimes he would be finished talking before we had started listening. He didn't rattle. I liked that and was proud of him for it, but I have to say too that it could be a burden. There would be times when he didn't have much to say about anything. If that lasted long enough, I began to feel his quietness as distance. There he would be—so

I would think to myself—outside love, outside marriage, way off by himself. Which of course left me by myself. Sometimes it would make me mad, and then I would make him mad. This was not something I did by deliberate intention but was just something I did. When we were both mad, we would have something to say to each other. It wasn't love, but it beat indifference, and sooner or later, mostly sooner, it would come to love.

Sometimes Nathan would do the same thing to me. We would get strayed apart somehow, he would get lonesome, and first thing you know he would do something to make me mad. I think husbands pick fights with their wives sometimes just to get their attention. If you can't get her hot, make her mad. You can't hold it against them. Or anyhow I can't, for as I've just confessed, I did it too.

Sometimes, too, Nathan's eagerness in his work would come across as nothing but impatience. That was his father in him. There were times when he was apt to run over you if you didn't get out of his way. He wasn't stubborn exactly, he was determined. There was a demand in him that you could feel. He didn't have to speak.

When I would be helping him with the cattle and would make a misstep and let one get by me, he would never say anything. He would just give me a look. Sometimes, doing that, he could make me so mad I could have shot him right between the eyes. He knew it too.

Once when I gave him his look back with interest, he laughed. He said, "Hannah, you'd be a bad hand to carry a pistol."

I didn't laugh. I stayed mad at him for about a day. And then finally he asked me, "Are you a pretty good shot with a pistol?"

"I couldn't hit the side of a barn," I said. "Lucky for you."

We both laughed then, and it was all right.

We had often enough the pleasure of making up, because we fell out often enough. But now, looking back, it is hard to say why we fell out, or what we fell out about, or why whatever we fell out about ever mattered. Even then it was sometimes hard to say.

One time we were fussing and Nathan looked at me right in the middle of it and said, "Hannah, what in the *hell* got us started on this?"

I said, "I *don't* know."

"Well, I don't know either," he said. "So I think I'm going to quit."

"Well, go ahead and quit," I said.

He said, "I already did." And that was the last word that time.

You have had this life and no other. You have had this life with this man and no other. What would it have been to have had a different life with a different man? You will never know. That makes the world forever a mystery, and you will just have to be content for it to be that way.

We quarreled because we loved each other, I have no doubt of that. We were trying to become somehow the same person, one flesh, and we often failed. When distance came between us, we would blame it on each other. And here is a wonder. I maybe never loved him so much or yearned toward him so much as when I was mad at him. It's not a simple thing, this love.

It wasn't always anger that came between us. Work could come between us. Thoughts could come between us. Feeling in different ways about the children could come between us. We would go apart, Nathan into whatever loneliness was his, I into mine. We would be like stars or planets in their orbits moving apart. And then we would come into alignment again, the sun and the moon and the earth. And then it would be as if we were coming together for the first time. It was like the time when I had decided that I would belong to whatever it was that we would be together, and I looked straight back at him at last. He would look at me with a grin that I knew. He would say, "Is it all right?" And I would say, "It's all right." The knowledge of his desire and of myself as desirable and of my desire would come over me. He would come to me as my guest, and I would be his welcomer.

What I was always reaching toward in him was his gentleness that had been made in him by loss and grief and suffering, a gentleness opposite to the war that he was not going to talk about, and never did, but that I know at least something about, having learned it since he died.

The gentleness I knew in him seemed to be calling out, and it was a gentleness in me that answered. That gentleness, calling and answering, giving and taking, brought us together. It brought us into the room of love. It made our place clear around us.

Nathan said, "You've seen those dragonflies flying together joined. How do they know to fly in the same direction?"

"They know," I said. "They know the same way we know."

That was what I wanted to say, and as I said it I realized it was what he wanted me to say.

It would be again like the coming of the rhymes in a song, a different song, this one, a long song, the rhymes sometimes wide apart, but the rhymes would come.

The rhymes came. But you may have a long journey to travel to meet somebody in the innermost inwardness and sweetness of that room. You can't get there just by wanting to, or just because the night falls. The meeting is prepared in the long day, in the work of years, in the keeping of faith, in kindness.

The room of love is another world. You go there wearing no watch, watching no clock. It is the world without end, so small that two people can hold it in their arms, and yet it is bigger than worlds on worlds, for it contains the longing of all things to be together, and to be at rest together. You come together to the day's end, weary and sore, troubled and afraid. You take it all into your arms, it goes away, and there you are where giving and taking are the same, and you live a little while entirely in a gift. The words have all been said, all permissions given, and you are free in the place that is the two of you together. What could be more heavenly than to have desire and satisfaction in the same room?

If you want to know why even in telling of trouble and sorrow I am giving thanks, this is why.

15

A Better Chance

Now that they are grown up and a long way gone, I am safe in saying that I had good children. I don't mean that they weren't lively and wide awake often enough when we were tired, or that they didn't make their share of messes and their share of mischief, or that they didn't cause us a fair amount of worry, or that they didn't sometimes sulk or complain or fight each other.

What I mean is that they accepted our love for them, and they loved us back. They did the work we needed for them to do, and mainly they learned to do it well. They never got into serious trouble away from home. They were good students and did well in school. Sometimes, now, I allow myself to wish that at least Caleb had not done so well in school.

I think I got off light. Heredity being what it is, I thought I might have to raise another Burley Coulter, and I'm glad to have been spared. Much as I have always loved him, it would have been hard to be his mother.

When they were young, I suppose all my thoughts about the children started with knowing they were mine. Because they were mine, I had to think of what I should do for them, of what Nathan and I could do for them to get them started in the world, of what they needed. Now all my thoughts about them start with knowing that they are gone.

They are gone. They come back varyingly often, and I remain attached to them, by love entirely, and partly by continuing knowledge. But the old ties, to be plain about it, are mostly broken. We live in different places, lead lives that are different, have different hopes and thoughts, know different things. We don't talk alike anymore.

I take some blame on myself for this. Maybe, given the times and fashions, it couldn't have happened in any other way. But I am sorry for my gullibility, my lack of foreknowledge, my foolish surprise at the way it turned out. Grandmam, who never went to high school, was desperate for me to go to high school. And I, who never went to college, was desperate for my children to go to college. Nathan, who also had never been to college, was less ambitious for the children than I was, but he agreed with me. We both wanted to send them to college, because we felt we owed it to them. That was the way we explained it to ourselves when we were saving the money and making the sacrifices it took to send them: "Well, we owe them that much. They're smart and they ought to go." It just never occurred to either of us that we would lose them that way. The way of education leads away from home. That is what we learned from our children's education.

The big idea of education, from first to last, is the idea of a better place. Not a better place where you are, because you want it to be better and have been to school and learned to make it better, but a better place somewhere else. In order to move up, you have got to move on. I didn't see this at first. And for a while after I knew it, I pretended I didn't. I didn't want it to be true.

But it was true. After they all were gone, I was mourning over them to Nathan. I said, "I just wanted them to have a better chance than I had."

Nathan said, "Don't complain about the chance you had," in the same way exactly that he used to tell the boys, "Don't cuss the weather." Sometimes you can say dreadful things without knowing it. Nathan understood this better than I did.

Like several of his one-sentence conversations, this one stuck in my mind and finally changed it. The change came too late, maybe, but it turned my mind inside out like a sock.

Was I sorry that I had known my parents and Grandmam and Ora Finley and the Catletts and the Feltners, and that I had married Virgil and come to live in Port William, and that I had lived on after Virgil's death to marry Nathan and come to our place to raise our family and live among the Coulters and the rest of our membership?

Well, that was the chance I had.

And so Nathan required me to think a thought that has stayed with me a long time and has traveled a long way. It passed through everything I know and changed it all. The chance you had is the life you've got. You can make complaints about what people, including you, make of their lives after they have got them, and about what people make of other people's lives, even about your children being gone, but you mustn't wish for another life. You mustn't want to be somebody else. What you must do is this: "Rejoice evermore. Pray without ceasing. In every thing give thanks." I am not all the way capable of so much, but those are the right instructions.

Here is my worry.

When they were little the children were always wanting stories. We read them stories and we told them stories. The stories they wanted most to be told were the stories of Nathan's childhood at Port William and mine at Shagbark.

"Tell us what you did when you were little."

"Tell us about the old days."

Well, the days before the war were "the old days," sure enough. The war changed the world. The days when Nathan and I were little, before we had electricity and plumbing and tractors and blacktopped roads and nuclear bombs, must have seemed almost legendary to the children, and so they were fascinated.

But did we tell the stories right? It was lovely, the telling and the listening, usually the last thing before bedtime. But did we tell the stories in such a way as to suggest that we had needed a better chance or a better life or a better place than we had?

I don't know, but I have had to ask. Suppose your stories, instead of mourning and rejoicing over the past, say that everything should have been different. Suppose you encourage or even just allow your children to believe that their parents ought to have been different people, with a better chance, born in a better place. Or suppose the stories you tell them allow them to believe, when they hear it from other people, that farming people are inferior and need to improve themselves by leaving the farm. Doesn't that finally unmake everything that has been made? Isn't that the loose thread that unravels the whole garment?

And how are you ever to know where the thread breaks, and when the tug begins?

Maybe it was because she was five years older than her oldest brother that Margaret always wanted to be a schoolteacher. If she hadn't really wanted to be a teacher, I guess she would have been badly discouraged by having her brothers as students. As soon as they were big enough to be played with, she would sit them in chairs and get behind a little table she had and teach them. It was a frustration from beginning to end. They were quick enough at learning, but they didn't want to learn anything from *her*. From the time they had minds of their own, she was always having to find them where they had hidden from her or run them down and catch them. And I would hear her saying things like "Children! May I have your attention?" Even so, for years her favorite play was to get somebody, even me, to pretend to be a student while she pretended to be a teacher. And so of course we expected that she would be a teacher when she grew up.

In looks she took after Mrs. Feltner maybe more than anybody. She was made like Mrs. Feltner, rather slight and fine. She was a pretty girl, with a good figure when she finally got one.

She was self-possessed and industrious, good-hearted and quiet, and plenty smart. In school she was always, I think, a sort of model student, as able to please as she was anxious to please. What people outside the family most often thought to call her was "a fine girl." She loved Nathan and got along with him so well that I sometimes envied him.

There was a passage of time when she and I got on each other's nerves and were often at outs. And it wasn't altogether her fault. I was as anxious about her as Grandmam had been about me. I knew she had sense, but I was afraid she wouldn't use it when she needed it. Even then, I think, I knew I was spending too much time telling her things she had already figured out for herself. But I couldn't bear not to tell her, and she couldn't bear to hear me. Later, when she finally was grown up and we were friends again, she said that what infuriated her the most was knowing she agreed with me.

When there was heat between us, and even when there wasn't, she would often ease away and take the path over to the Feltners'. They adored her, of course, and were always happy to see her—as in fact they were to see the boys when they came along. They would give her a big welcome and be really sweet to her, though they never in any way put themselves between her and me.

Their house had been her home for the first three years of her life, and of course it still felt like home to her. Going there restored something to her that she missed and needed. As long as the Feltners lived, her old bedroom was called "Little Margaret's room."

Another reason she went over there in those days was to get them to tell her stories about her dad. Mrs. Feltner would tell me of this, thinking I would want to know, and I did. It pleased me to know. I had always talked to her about Virgil, praising him to her, telling her things that made me happy to remember about our courtship and the brief time of our marriage. But I couldn't tell her as much as the Feltners could. After all, they had known him a lot longer than I had. They were his parents still, and I was no longer his wife.

I think that by sitting with them, letting them tell her stories about Virgil when he was a baby, when he was a boy, when he was a grown-up young man, she sort of came to know him. She was able to come into his presence, so to speak.

One evening after she had been over there, it was not long after she graduated from high school, I found her crying in her room, trying to keep me from hearing, but I had heard.

I said, "Honey, what's the matter?"

She had been lying face-down on her bed. When I spoke, she got up and came to me and hugged me. She said, "Oh, Momma!" And then a great grief came just tearing out of her. I had never heard her cry like that before, and I knew what had happened. They had been talking over there. Something had been said that had made Virgil's death real to her at last, and she was weeping for him, for her grandparents, for me, for herself.

I led her over to the rocking chair by the window and sat down and drew her onto my lap and held her and rocked her a long time while she cried and I cried. We wept it out together, she for the first time, I for the last, that old sorrow.

After that, we were two women. She took charge of herself. She grew up. We have been friends from then until now, though we have lived apart.

To be the mother of a grown-up child means that you don't have a child anymore, and that is sad. When the grown-up child leaves home, that is sadder. I wanted Margaret to go to college, but when she actually went away it broke my heart. Maybe if you had enough children you could get used to those departures, but, having only three, I never did. I felt them like amputations. Something I needed was missing. Sometimes, even now, when I come into this house and it sounds empty, before I think I will wonder, "Where are they?"

She went, like her brothers in their time, up to the university in Lexington. She had always liked writing letters, and she wrote to us and to her grandparents, a faithful girl. She would come home on the vacations. She was living already, and was preparing to live, in a different world from ours. But her goodness was that she kept on liking the world that she had come from. When she came home she just quietly went to work with us.

It is possible, as I know well, for farm-raised children to go to college and learn to be embarrassed by their parents and by their "rural background." Margaret never did. She was proud of us and kind to us. She brought her roommates and other friends home with her and showed Nathan and me and our place to them as proudly as if they had read about us in a book. Among her friends would sometimes be a boy, nothing serious.

And then, in the spring of her junior year, she began bringing Marcus. Or rather he began bringing her down here in his car. He was Marcus Settlemeyer. A nice boy. A nice young man. Good-looking and smart. He was from Louisville and knew nothing of such a life as ours, but he knew how to make himself at home with us. We liked him, which was made easy because he liked us. He was a year older than Margaret and a year ahead of her in school, but they had had some classes together and had got to know each other, and this time, if I knew the signs, it was serious.

One evening when they had come down for the Easter weekend, Margaret caught me by myself on the back porch. As she was apt to do, she just stood there smiling until I looked at her. When I did, she said, "Momma, don't you think Marcus and Margaret make a pretty sound together?"

The lightning flew through my heart, and for a minute I couldn't answer. And then I said, and I was surprised to hear Mrs. Feltner's voice in my own, "Honey, as long as they make a pretty sound to you, they'll sound pretty to me."

The next time she came home she was wearing his ring.

Marcus was planning to teach history and, he hoped, be a track coach in a high school. He graduated that spring and, sure enough, soon got the job he wanted at a school in Louisville. Margaret would stay in school in Lexington. They would wait to get married until she had finished. They were being sensible, and we were pleased. But we had seen the writing on the wall. Margaret was not going to come home.

The wedding, when the time for it came, made quite a commotion: two bridal showers, a lot of shopping and fixing, and the wedding itself. The first shower was given by some friends of Marcus's parents in a nice house on the outskirts of Louisville. For that and the wedding I got new dresses. Lyda Branch and Andy Catlett's wife Flora went to Louisville with me and helped me pick out two dresses that made me feel more splendid than anything I had had since the white-collared blue dress that Grandmam gave me to graduate in. When I wore the first one, the shower dress, Nathan shaded his eyes with his hand and said, "*Well now!*" And he gave me one of his better hugs.

The Louisville shower was for invited guests, Settlemeyer family and friends whose connections branched through the city like a nervous system. It was a very proper occasion, the house lovely and bright with cut flowers, the ladies all beautifully dressed, the gifts beautiful too, and everybody so kind and welcoming to Margaret that I kept having to look away and think of something else to keep from crying.

The Port William shower didn't distinguish the masses from the

classes, as Ernest Finley used to say. The invitation went out by announce-
ment at church and by hearsay. All the women could come who wanted
to, and it seemed that just about everybody wanted to. The shower was
in the dining room of the old Coulter home place, which is to say Lyda
Branch's house. At one end of the long table was a punch bowl and good
things to eat. At the other end Margaret sat in front of a pile of presents.
The ladies sat in chairs around all four walls. As Margaret opened the
presents, she held them up for everybody to see, and then they were
passed from hand to hand around the room. Some of the presents were
jokes: a baby potty with very realistic contents made by soaking graham
crackers in water, and a pair of knee-length blue silk drawers that Margaret must have opened six times because her friends kept re-wrapping
them and slipping them back into the pile. Others were remembrances
or reminders. Mrs. Feltner gave her a pair of embroidered pillowcases
made by Margaret's great-grandmother Feltner when she was still Nancy
Beechum, nearly a hundred years ago. They were handled around the
room as if they were living things.

The wedding was in the church in Port William with a reception afterwards in the basement. It was another event open to the general public,
at least as far as Port William was concerned. I have wondered sometimes if that was what Margaret really wanted. It may be that she
wanted it because she thought I wanted it, and I wanted it because I
thought she wanted it. Anyhow, it was a big wedding, and we made as
pretty a thing of it as we could.

Marcus said the crowd was "an interesting mix," and I guess it was.
There were the bridesmaids and the groomsmen, nifty, pretty kids in
their gowns and tuxedos. There were Marcus's family and friends from
Louisville and farther away. And from Port William there was Mrs. Feltner, needing to be helped along by her grandson Andy, and all the other
Catletts and all the Danny Branches and all the Grover Gibbses and Jayber Crow, the barber, and, it looked like, everybody else, all wearing
their Sunday clothes. And there was Burley Coulter wearing his ancient
blue suit and his only tie that he wore only on the most solemn occasions, a wide, bright red tie with a large yellow flower on it.

Ghosts attend such events. I don't know how else to say it. This was
1967. Mr. Feltner had been dead for two years, and Virgil for twenty-two.
You know the ghosts are there when you see as they see, not as they saw

but as they see. You feel them with you, not as they were but as they are. I never shed a tear that day, but all day long I saw Margaret as her father and her grandfather saw her. I loved her that day with my love but also with theirs. When I turned with the rest of the crowd to look and saw Nathan bringing her down the aisle, she smiling at Marcus waiting for her, and Nathan, I knew, wishing only to do well and go home, I saw her as Virgil and Mr. Feltner saw her, and I thought I would perish with the knowledge of loss and of having.

So Margaret married Marcus. They rented an apartment in Louisville, and Margaret got a job teaching the fifth grade. They would be one couple with two jobs, two incomes, and, if I'm not mistaken, two bank accounts. Margaret's school was a long way from Marcus's and in the opposite direction from their apartment. Because of that, she had to buy a car of her own right away. She borrowed the money to buy the car from the Independent Farmers Bank in Port William. The interest on the loan raised the cost of the car a lot higher than the sale price, and by the time she paid off the loan the worth of the car would be a lot less than she paid for it. In the meantime, they would have to pay for everything else they needed. Everything. I hadn't thought before of the fix they would be getting themselves into, but now that I did I was afraid for them. They were hardly going to be able to breathe without paying somebody for the privilege.

I said to Nathan, "They're starting out behind."

He didn't say anything. He just shook his head.

When we got married he had an old pickup truck that he had paid for with cash. It was a rattletrap, but we drove it until the children got so big we couldn't all sit in it. We had a debt on the farm, of course, for what seemed to us a lot of money in those days, but we went straight to work to make it worth more than Nathan had paid for it. We paid off that debt in nine years, and from then on, as Nathan liked to say, we never owed a nickel to anybody. We were paid up, living on our own land that was paid for, and so our work kept us.

You send your children to college, you do the best you can for them, and then, because you have to be, you're careful not to make plans for them. You don't want to be disappointed, and you don't want to burden them with your expectations either. But you keep a little thought, a little hope, that maybe they'll go away and study and learn and then come back, and you'll have them for neighbors. You'll have the comfort of being with them and having them for companions. You'll have your grandchildren nearby where you can get to know them and help to raise them. But that doesn't happen often anymore, and you know better than to hope too much. Or you ought to.

After each one of our children went away to the university, there always came a time when we would feel the distance opening to them, pulling them away. It was like sitting snug in the house, and a door is opened somewhere, and suddenly you feel a draft.

When Margaret set out to be a teacher, it was easy enough to think she might come home to teach. They had closed the school in Port William in 1964 and started taking the children to the new elementary school at Hargrave. Maybe, at least, she would end up no farther from home than Hargrave. But we knew it was iffy. More than likely she was going to marry somebody from away and would live away. That was expectable, and when it happened we weren't surprised. Having no choice but to let her go, we let her go, glad that she went no farther than Louisville.

16

M. B. Coulter ₀

With every year that passed it was getting less likely that a farmer's child was going to grow up to be a farmer. When our boys were still babies a great man in Washington was telling the farmers, "Get big or get out." The good farm economy that had held up through the war, and for a while after, began to weaken. By our hard work and investment we were going to be earning always a little less. It was going to get harder to farm and harder to expect your children to farm.

Mathew Burley Coulter, our Mattie, had the right middle name, I guess. With him, I came nearest to having a Burley Coulter to raise. He was a fun-loving boy, fine-looking, a little too attractive to girls when the time came for that, a little too eager to climb Fool's Hill. He had a wild streak in him, maybe, but it was my consolation that he could have been a lot wilder than he was. He could have been as wild as Burley Coulter, except for one thing: He had a mind that was studious. He could be attracted and pacified by the sort of things they teach in school. His interest ran to mathematics and science and to fixing things. From about the time he started into high school, whenever any of the equipment needed fixing, his daddy just handed it over to him.

He got good grades in school and satisfied his teachers, but what he learned seemed to have less and less to do with school. If there was something to be learned, especially in a subject he liked, he learned it. If they assigned him a textbook, he learned what was in it. But he was going ahead more or less on his own, just interested and eager.

At home he was a fascinating boy to be around and watch, he was so intent on what he was interested in and so good at it. As for farming, he did the work he was expected to do, and that was all. He did exactly what he was told to do, right up to the line, and no more. He wouldn't see work and do it on his own. Nathan would teach and prompt and occasionally plead and sometimes give him hell direct. But Mattie was looking away. He wasn't interested.

Nathan said, "I don't know what he's going to turn into. But he's not a farmer now and I'll be surprised if he ever is one."

Mattie was the only one of the three that Nathan and I ever really disagreed over. Nathan had good eyes and I trusted them, but I couldn't make myself care enough that Mattie should look with Nathan's eyes and see what he saw. Nathan cared plenty, and he could be awfully impatient and short with Mattie. Mattie dealt with this by getting away or, if he couldn't get away, by shutting up. They weren't always at odds, but when they were the space between them was occupied by, of course, me. And of course they complained to me about each other. And of course, loving them both, I tried to defend them to each other. The good part was that I *could* defend them to each other.

"Maybe *you* are the one who'll have to have the patience," I would say to Mattie. "Maybe you're the one who'll have to try harder. But your daddy loves you, you know. Whatever you're doing, right or wrong, and whatever you're thinking about him, he loves you."

That was the truth, and Mattie knew it. He wouldn't argue.

To Nathan I said, "I just think you need to be more patient with him. And with yourself too."

And he, who *would* argue, said, "All I want is to see that kid do one day's work because he wants to and not because he has to. That's the only difference I'm asking for, but it's one that matters."

"Well, maybe you've got to expect less. Or expect something else. He's not you. He's maybe never going to see what you see or want what you want."

"Then, damn it to hell, *you* deal with him."

"I *will* deal with him. I've dealt with him since before he was born, and I'm *going* to deal with him. And so are you. Listen, he's a good boy. He loves you, whether he shows it or not. And you love him. He's your *son.*"

Well, when Mattie finally grew all his feathers and flew off to the university, it broke my heart again, but it was a relief. I know it was a relief to him. And in different ways it was a relief to Nathan and me. It was *his* life that Mattie was living in after that, not ours. And once he was out from underfoot, Nathan was proud of him, for he did well.

He was proud of him but skeptical too, or maybe just sort of resigned. Mattie, anyhow, pretty quickly went beyond us. He studied electrical engineering, and then he got interested in communications technology and information technology, things he couldn't talk to us about because we knew so little.

Once, Nathan asked me, "Communication of *what?*"

I said, "God knows what."

And that was about the extent of our conversation on that subject. We didn't know what.

He was in graduate school a while, and then he lit out for the West Coast where he had been offered a high-paying, high-technological job. He was exceptional, and of course we were proud. But we were left behind too. We gave him up to whatever he was going to do.

He has been on the West Coast ever since. Now he is the CEO, as he puts it, of an information-processing company whose name is made of letters that don't spell anything. What he does I leave it to him to know. He is earning a lot of money and flying here and there about the world. He calls up maybe twice a month, but he doesn't come back often. Sometimes he sends a letter, usually a letter dictated to a secretary and signed, you can tell, with a bunch of other letters: "Very truly yours, M. B. Coulter." And I will laugh, for he is still going on in a hurry from one thing to another without looking back, the way he always did.

Once a year, maybe, he will bring his current family for a visit. It will be his vacation. Or rather part of his vacation. They fly to Cincinnati or Louisville, rent a car, and drive here on their way to or from someplace else.

I have this love for Mattie. It was formed in me as he himself was formed. It has his shape, you might say. He fits it. He fits into it as he fits into his clothes. He will always fit into it. When he gets out of the car and I meet him and hug him, there he is, him himself, something of my own forever, and my love for him goes all around him just as it did when he was a baby and a little boy and a young man grown.

He fits my love, but he no longer fits the place or our life or the knowledge of anything here. Since a long time ago, when he has come back he has come as a stranger. He and his wife and their children and I are strangers. We spend two or three days trying mightily to be nice to one another, and even succeeding, but we remain strangers. We don't know the same things. We have nothing in common to talk about. We don't always agree about the news, and so we avoid that. I ask about their lives, but they have little confidence that I can understand their lives, and they don't tell me much. The conversation, to keep itself going, keeps circling back to Port William, to things Mattie remembers, to people he used to know—memories, you can tell, that seem a little odd to him now, as if from another life—while his wife smiles and pretends to be interested, and the children play on the floor with the toys they have brought and pay no attention.

Mattie has four children by two wives, and between those two there was another woman he was at least traveling with. All Nathan and I ever knew of her was what Mattie told us when he introduced her: "Folks, this is Helen."

Though we kept on calling him "Mattie," and I still do, the name fits him as poorly now as he fits this place. We have no other name for him, but he doesn't look right for the name. He looks like somebody expecting to be called "Mr. Coulter." His present wife calls him "M.B."

He has too much honesty to pretend to be interested in whatever is happening here on the place. Farming is behind him now, and it is completely behind him. He was always looking away, and now when he is here it appears really that he doesn't see where he is. His children, as they have come along, have picked this up from him. When they are here they don't know where they are. And maybe it is not possible for them to find out. They don't want to know.

The oldest pair of Mattie's children are grown up now, and I haven't seen them for a long time. The youngest pair, two boys, are now twelve and thirteen. Like their older brother and sister, they would spend their whole visit in the house or on the porch if I would let them. They bring games that they play on the little computer they always have with them. They play their games or they sit and watch television. Before they come and while they're here I think of things to show them: a new calf, a hawk's nest, the old hollow tree. I take them fishing in the ponds. I take them out to help me in the garden or the henhouse. I send them out to see whatever the Branches are doing. It all somehow fails. They don't much like any of it. By no fault of theirs, they don't know enough to like it. They don't know the things that I and even their daddy have known since before we knew anything.

And what ever in their lives will they think of the old woman they will barely remember who yearned toward them and longed to teach them to know her a little and who wanted to give them more hugs and kisses than she ever was able to?

My love for Mattie's children was made in my love for Mattie, but it was also made in Port William. It doesn't fit the children, who had their making elsewhere, and they don't fit it. It is a failed love, and hard to bear. For me, it is hard to bear. The children don't notice, of course, and don't mind.

When they leave I am sad to see them go, and I am sad that it should seem right that they should be gone.

17
Caleb

Margaret was a bright girl, a top student, and she has always had plenty of sense. Mattie has always had the reputation of being "brilliant," and maybe he is. Maybe he has made enough money to prove it. But I am not a good authority on Mattie. He has gone beyond about everything I know. I don't know if I am right or wrong in wishing, as I sometimes do, that he had more sense.

The tale of Caleb is maybe the most complicated of the three. As a boy Caleb never wanted to be in school, though he has wound up in school for life, or at least for life until retirement. I am not sure how smart Caleb is. He is not "brilliant," maybe, and yet he seems always to have been as smart as he has wanted to be.

He didn't want to be in school, when he was a boy, because he wanted to be here, at home. He wanted to be at work with his daddy, which he was, on every day that Nathan would let him come along, from the time he could walk until he started to school. Nathan had more to do with raising Caleb than I did. I would have made a momma's boy of him, maybe, if he had let me. He was the last. But his natural calling, I think, was to be a farmer. Farming was what he played at before he could work at it. When he got big enough to work, he liked the work. Farming was what he thought about and dreamed about. He loved it. When Mattie would be doing what was expected of him, no more, and getting away, Caleb would do his work and then look around for something else that needed to be done.

When he was just a little thing, if the work permitted it, he would be out with his dad, and maybe Jarrat and Burley too, trying to do as they did. If he got sleepy, Nathan would put him down for a nap at the field edge or on the seat of his pickup, or if the weather was too bad for that, he would come carrying him back to the house asleep. When he was supposed to be staying at the house with me, if I didn't watch, he would run away to find the men at work. Before he started to school he knew this farm as he knew the inside of his clothes.

He was the one who raised the orphan lambs. He always wanted to have his own hen and chickens. Nathan would give him the runt pigs, and he would feed and care for them in his own pen. He had a bank account by the time he was nine. When he was fourteen, we gave him an acre of tobacco to raise for himself. He dealt with school the way Mattie dealt with the farm, doing what was required and no more, except for the agriculture courses and the Future Farmers of America. He loved to have "projects." He did his schoolwork without too much effort, made his C's and a few B's as if they were exactly what he wanted, caused probably only a normal amount of trouble, fell in and out of love with a girl or two, but the school he was really interested in attending was here. He was his daddy's student. He never thought of being anything but a farmer.

So our hope that we might give this place a true inheritor and ourselves a successor naturally fell on Caleb. You could say even that he invited our hope and gladly accepted it. He was a sweet-natured boy, kind-hearted and generous, and I think he liked the thought of pleasing us. When his time came to go up to the university, his plan was to study agriculture and come home to farm.

He was the youngest, the last, and I hated to see him go. I loved him, I guess, the way mothers usually love their youngest, and he was easy to love, but I was worried about him too. He had been so uninterested and unworried in his schooling so far that I was afraid he would go into those high-powered classes at the university and fail.

I caught him by himself when he was getting ready to leave and laid down the law, which I hadn't needed to do with either of the others. I said, "Listen. Don't go up there and try to get by with a lick and a promise. You're going up there to study, so study. If you do badly the first semester, don't expect us to help you with the next one."

Not every boy would have taken that in a good spirit. Mattie wouldn't have. But Caleb tried to console me. He said, "Momma, don't worry," and gave me a very kind hug.

Anytime an eighteen-year-old boy tells you not to worry, you had better worry. And I did. As it turned out, though, I was wasting my time. Caleb went up there and became what he had never been before, a good student. He made whatever struggle he had to make. His grades were decent at first, and they got better as he went along.

When the distance began to open up for Caleb I am not quite sure. He got a scholarship in the college of agriculture. Because of research projects that he was helping with, his visits home became shorter. In the summer before his senior year he didn't come home. I began to have this uneasy feeling that he was doing too well. I felt so foolish in that thought that I didn't mention it to Nathan. I barely had the nerve to mention it to myself.

Oftentimes after it no longer matters whether things are clear or not, they become clear. After not liking school at all, Caleb had got to liking it too much, more anyhow than I would have wanted him to, if I had had any say. He liked knowing the things he was learning. He was beginning to learn the ways of research, and he liked that. He was, maybe you could say, tempted by it.

And I know, I can almost hear, the voices that were speaking to him, voices of people he had learned to respect, and they were saying, "Caleb, you're too bright to be a farmer."

They were saying, "Caleb, there's no future for you in farming."

They were saying, "Caleb, why should you be a farmer yourself when you can do so much for farmers? You can be a help to your people."

These were the voices of farm-raised people who were saying, "Caleb, why go home and work your ass off for what you'll earn? Things are going to get worse for farmers." And they were true prophets. The farmers were at the bottom of the heap. And there were fewer of them, farming worse and earning less every year. How could you argue with those voices? How could you look straight at your boy and argue that he ought to spend his life at the hardest work, worrying about money and the weather?

I don't think there is an argument for being a farmer. There are only two reasons to farm: because you have to, and because you love to. The ones who choose to farm choose for love. Necessity ends the argument, and so does love. Caleb didn't need to farm. Going to school had removed the need. With the need gone, he still had love, but he didn't have enough. Once again, I had felt the distance opening. I had seen the writing on the wall. And Nathan ought to have seen it. I should have helped him to see it.

Caleb came home the day after he graduated. And that day Nathan did the only really foolish thing I ever saw him do. I didn't see it coming. I didn't know it was going to happen until it had already started happening, and I couldn't help.

Nathan came to the house for dinner just at noon, the way he always did. He hung his hat on the hook by the back door and washed his hands at the sink. I took up the biscuits, and the three of us, Nathan and Caleb and I, sat down in our old places to eat.

Nobody said much of anything for a few minutes, and then Nathan looked across the table at Caleb with that point-blank look he had when there was something to be dealt with. He said, "Caleb, we've talked before, and now it's time to talk again. I've been thinking about what we have to offer you here, and what we can do for you."

All of a sudden I knew a lot more than I had thought I did. Nathan had fooled himself, and he was afraid he had fooled himself, and now he was begging Caleb to tell him that he hadn't fooled himself. The cold ache of dread settled into the pit of my stomach, and I laid down my fork.

"There's this place here," Nathan said. "Your mother and I aren't going to live forever. Sooner or later it's going to need a younger man. And there's your sister's place that I'm taking care of; it can use a younger man right now. And there's my daddy's little place that was left to me; that can be yours just as soon as we can make the arrangements. Sooner or later you'll want to get married, and when you do, we can fix up the old house over there. It'll be your place. Later, maybe, you'll want to move here."

Caleb had turned white. He had raised his glass but he had not carried it all the way to his mouth. He set it back down. Poor boy. He had changed his mind, and he hadn't told us. He had put it off, thinking it would become easy. He would think of a way to make it easy. He hoped we would figure it out.

When he spoke, he sounded alarmed, as if only then he realized what he had to tell. "But, Dad, I'm not here to stay. I'm not going to be coming home. I've been offered a scholarship to a graduate school. I've accepted."

There was nothing more to say, Caleb didn't need a graduate degree to be a farmer, and Nathan didn't say anything. He went on eating. He had his work to do, and he needed to get back to it. Tears filled his eyes and overflowed and ran down. I don't think he noticed he was crying.

That was as near to licked as I ever saw him. Even his death didn't come as near to beating him as that did. Afterwards, for a long time he was just awfully quiet. He wasn't angry. Really, he was never much for anger. But it was a hard time. He had lost something he needed, something his place and his family needed. That was 1974. Elton Penn had died that spring, and we were already grieved. Nathan had more on his mind than he could find words for. So did I. I would talk to him, and he would answer pleasantly enough, but we didn't speak of what was bothering us the most. Maybe we didn't need to. It couldn't have been "talked out." It had to be worn out. But all through that time I had an absurd yearning to shelter Nathan from what had already happened.

Troubled about himself, I think, and sorry for his dad and for me, Caleb lived at home and helped us through that summer. Before the crop was all in the barn, he left for his graduate school in the Midwest.

And so they were gone, all three. And so they still are gone.

For a while, especially if you have children, you shape your life according to expectations. That is arguably pretty foolish, for expectation can be a bucketful of smoke. Nobody expected Elton to die. He was only fifty-four. Nobody expected Caleb, who loved to farm, to spend his life in school. But there is some pleasure in expectations too, and I should not be regretful about ours.

After your expectations have gone their way and your future is getting along the best it can as an honest blank, you shape your life according to what it is. Nathan was fifty in 1974. He was probably as strong as he had ever been, and I would say smarter. He had a lot of years still ahead of him. *We* had a lot of years still ahead of *us*. It was up to us then to make them good, and we did.

One night, after Caleb had left and we had got well into the fall, Nathan and I were sitting at the table after supper. We were tired. Neither of us had said anything for a long time. It had got dark but we hadn't turned on a light.

And then Nathan said, "Hannah, my old girl, we're going to live right on. We'll love each other, and take care of things here, and we'll be all right."

"Yes," I said. "We're going to love each other, and we'll be all right."

I got up and went to him then.

And what of Caleb? Caleb eventually became Dr. Coulter. He became a professor, teaching agriculture to fewer and fewer students who were actually going to farm. He became an expert with a laboratory and experimental plots, a man of reputation.

But as I know, and as he knows in his own heart and thoughts, Caleb is incomplete. He didn't love farming enough to be a farmer, much as he loved it, but he loved it too much to be entirely happy doing anything else. He is disappointed in himself. He is regretful in some dark passage of his mind that he thinks only he knows about, but he can't hide it from his mother. I can see it in his face as plain as writing. There is the same kind of apology in him that you see in some of the sweeter drunks. He is always trying to make up the difference between the life he has and the life he imagines he might have had.

He can leave his office on Friday afternoon and drive here in just a few hours, and then drive back again in just a few hours on Sunday afternoon. He often has done that, almost from the time he took his present job. Every chance he got, it seemed, he would be here, if only just overnight, or for only a few hours on his way someplace else or on his way home, to see how we were and if he could do anything for us. Since his daddy's death, he has come more often than before. Too often, I try to tell him, for a married man with a job and responsibilities.

Maybe it was because of his feeling of unfinished responsibilities here that he didn't marry until he was thirty-four. He married Alice Hamilton, who goes by that name. She is a vice president in a pretty large bank. I like her. As a rule, she knows what she thinks and means what she says. She is self-respecting and courteous. She appreciates Caleb's goodness, which she ought to do, and she is kind to me. She sometimes comes here with Caleb on his visits, but not often. And sometimes she says things to the effect that you can take the boy out of the country but you can't take the country out of the boy, which I *don't* like. I gather that with her and their circle of friends, Caleb enjoys the reputation of being a country boy. He is Alice's boy. They have no children.

They both have done well, and they live well. Caleb is well respected, and I am glad of that. He brings me what he calls his "publications," written in the Unknown Tongue. He wants me to be proud of them. And I am, but with the sadness of wishing I could be prouder.

I read all of his publications that he brings me, and I have to say that they don't make me happy. I can't hear Caleb talking in them. And they speak of everything according to its general classification. Reading them always makes me think of this farm and how it has emerged, out of "agriculture" and its "soil types" and its collection of "species," as itself, our place, a place like no other, yielding to Nathan and me a life like no other.

One of the things that Nathan disliked and feared the most was even the idea of being an employee. Except for his time in the army, he was never "employed" in his life, and he would do everything he could to avoid employing anybody. He hated the idea of working for a boss, and he hated being a boss. Freedom, to him, was being free of being bossed and of being a boss.

He loved the old free work-swapping with our kinfolks and friends, who needed no bossing but out of their regard and respect for one another did what they were supposed to do. When we would have to hire somebody, as we sometimes did, and he proved unsatisfactory, as he usually did, Nathan would say, "Another damned employee." And that was the harshest criticism he ever made of the children: "You're acting like a damned employee."

He quit saying such things after Margaret became an employee of her school board and Mattie an employee of his company and Caleb an employee of his university, but I know he kept thinking them. He wanted to be free himself, and he wanted his children to be free.

Because of the same desire, I suppose, I sometimes allow myself to wonder if Caleb might not wind up here after all. He is forty-eight years old now. He doesn't know it yet, but it won't be a long time before he is going to begin to think of retirement, of where he will live out the rest of his life, of where he will die. I think he might want to come home then, having been homesick for most of his life. I think he might consider it. But that may be another bucket of smoke, better not thought of. Alice and her wants will have to be considered too, and the changing of the world. And what would he do here as an old man, after such a life, if he came back?

Way leads on to way, as the poet says, and what is done is hard to undo. And yet love is not satisfied with such answers but remembers and endures all things and yearns across the distances. As long as the children have been away, I still wonder about them, and I worry.

"I worry," I said to Andy Catlett, "because I don't know what is going to become of them. At the end, I mean."

He nodded. He knew what I meant. It used to be that we sort of knew, we could sort of guess, how the lives closest to us would end, what beds our dearest ones were likely to die in, and who would be with them at the last. Now, in this world of employees, of jobs and careers, there is no way even to imagine.

Andy said, "You're worried because they've left the membership," and he smiled, knowing we both knew whose word that was. "They've gone over from the world of membership to the world of organization. Nathan would say the world of employment."

And I said, "Yes. That's the trouble I have in mind."

One of the attractions of moving away into the life of employment, I think, is being disconnected and free, unbothered by membership. It is a life of beginnings without memories, but it is a life too that ends without being remembered. The life of membership with all its cumbers is traded away for the life of employment that makes itself free by forgetting you clean as a whistle when you are not of any more use. When they get to retirement age, Margaret and Mattie and Caleb will be cast out of place and out of mind like worn-out replaceable parts, to be alone at the last maybe and soon forgotten.

"But the membership," Andy said, "keeps the memories even of horses and mules and milk cows and dogs."

Caleb, anyhow, was the last of the three ever to live at home. When he was gone the nest, as they say, was empty, and that was something to be sad about. But not entirely. It was lovely after so many years to be living alone with Nathan. We were living right on. We were working hard. And yet, as Nathan said, we were "playing house" too. It was the old happiness of nobody looking, only now nobody was looking almost all the time. We got so we would be very free with looks and touches and kisses and hugs. Anybody young would have laughed at us, but now nobody young was here.

The only people here were just this aging couple, getting a little too small for their skin, their hair turning white, standing it might be in the middle of the kitchen or the garden or the barn lot, hugging each other the way the hungry eat, in a hurry for night to fall. We still had the children to think about and worry about, of course, wherever they were, and our work always ahead of us, and the place always around us with its needs and demands, and yet for a while there I would think that this, this right now, was all the world that I held in my arms. It was like falling in love, only more than that; we knew too much by then for it to be only that. It was knowing that love was what it was, and life would not complete it and death would not stop it. While we held each other and our old desire came upon us, eternity flew into time like a lighting dove.

18

Margaret

Burley Coulter used to describe as "wayward" the descent of parcels of land through the generations. I have seen for myself that the descent is wayward. The ideal, I suppose, would be for every farm to be inherited by a child who grew up on it, and who then would live on it and farm it and care well for it in preparation for the next inheritor. But it has not always been that way, and from the end of World War II it seems to have been that way less and less.

Mrs. Feltner lived on for nearly five years after Mr. Feltner died. She was bedfast for about a year at the last. But her mind stayed alert and lively, and from her bedroom windows she kept constant watch on the road and on the driveway going back past the house to the barn. Until she died, everybody had the feeling of being watched over, and we knew we would have to account for ourselves.

I would go in over there and she would already have seen me coming, or she would have recognized my steps in the kitchen, and she would be waiting for me. "Honey, I saw Nathan come in a while ago with his tractor and wagon. Are they getting ready to bale the hay? Tell me what everybody's doing."

Or Andy Catlett would come in. "Honey, I saw you go by early this morning. Were you going to Hargrave? Sit down a minute, and tell Granny what you've been doing."

She wasn't supervising or being nosey. She was one of us still. If we were doing all right, she wanted to be pleased. If we were worried or troubled, she wanted to be worried or troubled with us. After she died, I kept for a long time the feeling of being watched over by her. Andy says that he has never lost his feeling of being somehow accountable to her. As long as she was alive, her house was the focus of the farm, and her bedroom was the focus of the house. After she died, things seemed to go out of focus for a while, and I felt strange to myself. I had known her, I might as well say I had been her daughter, for twenty-eight years. In my time of greatest need she had given me her love and her kindness and her welcome, and once she had given them she never took them back. For a while after she was gone, I felt off-balance, as if I needed to learn again how to stand alone.

The Feltners' estate was settled by Wheeler Catlett. There were two heirs: Wheeler's wife, Bess, and my Margaret. After some careful discussion, at first between Wheeler and Bess as I imagine, and then between Wheeler and Bess and Margaret and Nathan and me, the money and bank stock went to Bess, and the farm, with some debt to Bess, went to Margaret.

It might have worked out that way without Wheeler, but I think the arrangement had his mark on it, and I know it was to his liking. I know pretty well how he thought about it. He would not have wanted to see the land divided. He would have wanted the farm to go intact to one heir, preferably to one of the grandchildren, for that would have promised the longest holding by the family. Bess had no need or use for a farm, and both of the Catlett boys, who by then had settled here, already had farms of their own. Henry was on the Catlett home place out on the Bird's Branch Road, and Andy was on the old Riley Harford place on Harford Run above Katy's Branch. The next in line was Margaret, who had no more need or use for a farm than Bess, but she was younger than Bess by thirty-seven years. Wheeler was not a great hand to depend on the future, but he would do it if he had to. "If you know you don't know anything about the future," he would say, "and if you believe that with

God all things are possible, then you have to think that something good may happen." The future would be a gamble, and Wheeler, having no choice, took the gamble.

He told me afterwards, "Well, she's got her place. If she ever wants to come to it, she'll have it. It's more hers, anyhow, than that apartment she's living in." I knew he didn't mean just that it was legally hers. He meant also that it was hers because it would have been Virgil's. Wheeler was a man who held himself answerable to the dead. That the place was now Margaret's was a justice owed, and now paid, to Virgil.

I was afraid to think that Margaret might ever come home to live. But I knew that the ownership of that farm put such a possibility ahead of us for somebody, if somebody would ever want it, and so I accepted the gamble in the same spirit that Wheeler did. And it was a comfort to me to know that Margaret would own the old place that she would think of as home whether she owned it or not, the place that would have been her father's and mine if he had lived.

Margaret is smart, and she has sense. Marcus has sense too, or he did for a while. Margaret's inheritance of the Feltner place along with her debt to her aunt Bess seemed to make them more thoughtful and careful than they had been. They had enough equity in the farm to finance the purchase of a house in Louisville if they had decided to do that. Instead of paying rent then, they would have been buying something of worth that would belong to them. But Margaret said, "I don't want to put the farm in danger to buy a house. I don't want to owe money on everything we have." Marcus agreed, and so they stayed in their apartment until the farm was cleared of debt. And maybe, in her mind, that too was a justice to Virgil.

Even as an apartment-dweller in the city, Margaret was a thrifty, practical woman. Whenever she came up here, she would pitch in with me or with Nathan and me at whatever we were doing. In the summer she would come out and help in the garden, Marcus too sometimes, and we would can and preserve for both households. She was the only one of the children close enough for us to help in that way, and it was a pleasure. We would pass along surpluses of cream and butter and eggs, and send fresh sausage and tenderloin and a ham or two when we killed hogs.

They bought a house finally in 1975, and their only child, a boy, Virgil Feltner Settlemeyer, was born a year later. Virgie, as we called him, is the only one of the grandchildren who has lived close enough to get to know. We visited back and forth pretty often. Virgie called us Grandmam and Grandpap. He loved to see us coming when we visited down there, and he always lit here excited. When he got old enough we kept him here with us sometimes for weeks at a stretch. Following me to the henhouse and garden, or going to the fields with Nathan, or wandering about by himself, he learned some of the things I wanted him to know.

It got so we saw a good deal more of Virgie than we did of Margaret and Marcus. They had their own house and yard and garden to look after, they were busier at work, and they were giving more time to their social life. We still had a connection, but it wasn't what it had been. It was less practical. More and more, the connection was Virgie.

And we continued to be connected by the Feltner place. Nathan had been the Feltner's tenant over there, and he continued as Margaret's tenant, though of course he was a lot more than that. He was her partner and farm manager and adviser and teacher and friend—a father to her, in fact, just as he had always been. And they got along. Under an absentee owner, a farm usually runs down, but neither Margaret nor Nathan would let that happen. Margaret willingly spent what was needed to take good care of it, and Nathan willingly went to the trouble and did the work. The farm has stayed in good shape to this day. Danny Branch has been a good and faithful successor to Nathan.

Only the old house is suffering. Margaret hasn't slighted it. She has kept it painted and repaired, has kept the weather out of it. But the people who rent houses in Port William now are commuters who come here to live because they can't find "a better place." They usually don't intend to stay long, and usually they don't. And so the house suffers not only the wear of use, but also the wear of indifference. When love for a place is not living in it, you will know just by driving by it on the road. This is hard on Margaret, and on me too. It was hard on Nathan. There have been chances to divide the house from the farm and sell it to people who maybe would have lived in it a long time and taken care of it, but Margaret has let those slip by. I am not sure what she had in mind, or even what Nathan had in his. I know what I had in my mind. What I had in my mind, God help me, was the thought that some day Virgie might want the place for himself, and would come there and fix the house up and renew it and live in it with a wife and children, and would bring the old memories home again, and give them a proper dwelling place. I suppose the others were thinking the same thing, but maybe not. If they were, maybe we all ought to have been more careful. But at least we weren't hoping out loud. We weren't allowing our hopes to become expectations.

Expectations are tempting, pleasant, maybe necessary. They are scary too, once you have had some experience. They are not necessarily and not always a bucket of smoke, but they can be and are even likely to be. A lot depends on keeping the prospect open. For Virgie, the prospect, at least in this direction, began to close before he was born.

As a farm owner, Margaret was in a pretty tilty situation. She was gone from her place. She was not living in it and thinking about it every day, which meant that Virgie, however often he came to it as a visitor and a guest, was gone from it too. He grew up without any idea what it is to live in a place and think about it and do its work and worry about it and love it and admire it every day the year around.

As a woman living in the modern world, Margaret's situation was also pretty tilty. I had thought it was, but it turned out to be more tilty than I had thought.

She and Marcus were working in different places, going off every morning in opposite directions. They worked apart, worked with different people, made friends with different people. What they had in common to hold them together were Virgie, their house, and the weekends. Margaret was still attached to Port William, not attached enough for the good of the Feltner place, and too much attached maybe for the good of Marcus and her marriage.

How can you know what goes on inside of somebody else's marriage? You know what you see from the outside. You know what you're told.

I know it was one of the earliest warm evenings in the spring of 1988. I had come out to sit on the front porch and look at the woods along the creek turning soft and green with young leaves. The cows with their new calves had just been turned into the front pasture, and they were grazing down by the spring. Nathan hadn't come in for supper yet and probably wouldn't until after dark. He was trying to finish planting corn before it rained. I could hear his tractor running up on the ridge behind the house.

I heard a car come over the hill, slow down, and turn into our lane. When it came out of the woods, I recognized it. It was Margaret's, and I knew that something wasn't right. It was a Tuesday, the wrong day for her to be out here.

She drove on up past the house to park in the back as she usually did, and I went through the house to meet her. I came out into the backyard just as she was getting out of the car. Her face told me again that something was not right, and out of my old uneasiness about her I said, "Where's Marcus?"

She had come to tell me. It was her duty to tell me, and she needed the comfort of telling me. Her face told me that she had it all composed into a little speech. She was not going to burden me with her feelings, just with her news.

But she could manage only one word, "Gone," and then I was holding my daughter all in pieces in my arms.

Marcus had fallen in love with another woman. A younger woman, of course, one of the teachers in his school. It had happened, Marcus said, because "it wanted to happen." Not because he wanted it to happen, of course. He had rented an apartment, and that day had moved out of the house. He had asked for a divorce. I led her into the kitchen and we sat down at the table.

I said, "Where's Virgie?"

"Staying with one of his friends," she said. "He doesn't know yet. When he comes home from school tomorrow, I'll have to tell him."

I wanted to say something bad about Marcus, and I was about to say it when I realized I mustn't, because I realized at the same time that Margaret mustn't. We couldn't turn Virgie against his father. The most important person in this was going to be Virgie. We were going to have to keep him free of our judgment of Marcus.

It had got dark. We heard the tractor coming down to the barn. We had finished crying by then, both of us, and we hurried now, laughing at ourselves, to get the look of crying off our faces before Nathan came in.

He came in, tired, with the dust of the field on him, but alert and anxious, having seen Margaret's car. She stood and went to him to get her hug. He looked at me, asking me to tell him what was wrong, not wanting her to have to do it, and I told him while he held her and patted her shoulder.

I never was so grateful to him. I told him in about two sentences. When I was finished he nodded. He said, "Honey, let's sit down."

She sat down again at the end of the table, where she had been before, and he sat beside her, just the corner of the table between them. He took her hand. He said, "Margaret, my good Margaret, we're going to live right on."

I heard him say that only three or four times in all his life. He said it only when he knew that living right on was going to be hard. Her eyes were dry by then, but his had tears in them.

He started talking to her about the future. She could come home. She could come back to her own place. She could be here with us, who loved her. Virgie would have a place here where he would belong, and where he would always know he belonged.

I don't know that any of us believed in that future. Distance and difference had come between us, and we all knew it. But it was a possible future, and it was a gift. It signified to her that she could think beyond that day, that the world extended beyond any line that Marcus had drawn or could draw, that life was still generous, that she had in fact a life to live.

None of us were surprised, I think, that Margaret did not choose the future that Nathan spoke of that night. Maybe she could not have chosen it. She was forty-three that year. Her life had a shape and a direction by then that would have been hard to change. More was involved of course than Nathan and I would ever know. But as it turned out, we did give Virgie a place to belong, when he most needed to belong somewhere, and maybe too a place where he will always know he belongs.

It seems strange to me that Nathan, who I am very sure had killed people in the war, seemed never to nourish anger in his mind, but I, who have never killed anything that I wasn't going to eat, except flies, have sometimes had thoughts that were perfectly murderous. I wanted to go to work on Marcus with a two-handed piss-ellum club, and I wanted him to know I was going to hit him a good while before I hit him.

I would go about muttering in my mind things I enjoyed muttering and that I wished Marcus could have overheard. "Ordinarily you can't turn a frog into a prince by kissing it," I would think. "So girls oughtn't to marry frogs."

But Marcus, as I well knew, was not a frog. Marcus, in fact, had been pretty well what the recipe called for: handsome, smart, well-mannered, from a nice family, a promising young man in every way. So how come he ended up leaving his wife and boy, talking about "fulfillment" and his "need to be free"? "It's the time," I thought. "The time wants men to be as silly in character as they are by nature."

It is easy enough for a woman to feel threatened by a man's manly instincts, once she knows what they are. And a woman's womanly instincts are no better. Men don't usually leave their wives for the pleasure of solitude. A man's desire is the most flattering mirror a woman ever stands before, and she wants to see herself shining in it. But after Marcus left Margaret rejected and alone and Virgie mostly without a daddy exactly when he most needed one, I kept fuming in my mind about men. I could hardly stop long enough to fume about Marcus's girlfriend, soon enough his bride.

One night I said to Nathan, "What are we going to be, just a bunch of livestock? Are the men just going to breed from one to the next like buck sheep?"

In my anger, I thought he might offer some kind of apology for the nature of men or, even better, defend it. I was ready for a fight.

But of course he didn't do either one. He was reading the paper, and for maybe a minute he went on reading it. And then he laid it on his lap and folded it up, looking straight at me the way he would do. He said, "That would take a world of time and trouble, Hannah. It would have been better for Marcus if he had been tireder at night."

Nathan was a rock for me when I needed one, and when Virgie needed one he was a rock for Virgie. When he was little, Virgie liked to come to stay with us. After his parents divorced, he began needing to come. He was big enough by then to be of some help, and he wanted to help. It was help that Nathan was glad enough to have. He was glad of the company too, I know. He paid Virgie a fair wage, and the two of them would be together at work all day. For a long time Virgie would come to stay with us every chance he got, every holiday, most weekends, and all summer. It was a joy to me to be cooking again for a hungry boy, and I too was glad of his company.

At the time Virgie started seriously working for Nathan he was getting to be a big boy, but he had a lot of growing still to do. He was at the age when he was neither a boy nor a man. He looked somehow out of place everywhere, even in his own clothes. He was so eager to do well and to please that sometimes he overdid it, went too fast, and screwed things up or broke something. He was a quiet boy, hardly more talkative than Nathan, but was watching us all the time to see if he was doing all right, if we approved of him. Which usually we did.

He and Nathan made an odd team, a boy with energy to spare and an aging man with only enough. "I can barely stay with him," Nathan would tell me in front of Virgie. "He's about to leave me in the dust." And Virgie, trying not to look proud, would look so proud that we could have laughed if we had let ourselves.

He was always doing something like that, something boyish and awkward and tender and exposed, that made me want to hug him. And when I wanted to, I did. He was always very willing to be hugged. And I would see Nathan standing with his arm around him in order to tell him something or reaching out to give him a pat.

To this day, I don't know what Nathan expected Virgie to turn out to be. Virgie's future was not a subject we talked about. Caleb, I think, had pretty well cured Nathan of forming expectations about the futures of other people. But of Virgie in the present, I know he expected a good deal. He expected him to stay at his work and do it right. Virgie was willing enough to do both, but when he was wrong, Nathan would correct him. I can hear him now: "Whoa, Virgie! That's not the way. Use your head, now." And Virgie was making a good hand. He was learning to be a farmer, and he was proud of himself.

Nathan might as well have been Virgie's own grandfather, just as he himself might as well have been the Feltners' son. Virgie was receiving from Nathan about the same handed-down love that he would have received from Virgil, if Virgil had lived. And Nathan's love for Virgie didn't have any of the strictness that often gets into fathers' love for their sons, that got into Nathan's love for his own sons, out of his fear for them. Maybe Nathan really was withholding all expectations from Virgie's future. Virgie, anyhow, felt free with him, and he loved him as maybe a boy can only love his grandfather.

At first, when Virgie came out for a stay, Margaret would bring him, or, if Nathan or I had to be in Louisville for something, we would bring him home with us. He came, either way, with his mother's permission. And then, after the divorce, as the hard days of his growing up came on him, he began showing up here sometimes without her permission. He would be at odds with his teachers or with Marcus or both, which would sooner or later put him at odds with his mother. And then, feeling friendless and ill-at-home in Louisville, he would put out his thumb and catch a ride, or several rides, to Port William, missing usually a day of school in the process. Nathan would have to pat him down, like bread dough that was rising too fast, and take him back home.

And then Virgie pretty much quit coming out here at all. It was, I guess, predictable enough. First came girls, and then a town job after school and on weekends, and then a car, and then other things that I know even less about. With all their energy to spend, and especially now, the young live several lives. They live out of one life and into another as easily as they ever grew out of their clothes. That is wonderful, but it is dangerous. For a while, this place and working with Nathan were all the world to Virgie, and then his life in Louisville became his world.

His parents tried to keep him in his old life and ways. Margaret, I think might have done it, for she was pretty sensible and steady with him. But she failed. She failed, partly at least, because her wishes for Virgie were the same as Marcus's, and Virgie had turned hard against Marcus. They mainly wanted him to do well in school, and they were against some things—the job, going out too much at night—because they distracted him from school. And if Virgie had to defy his mother in order to defy his father, he was willing to do it. After all, he was just a boy.

Margaret and Nathan and I had all been careful enough, I think, to shelter Virgie from our opinions of Marcus, but Virgie had got old enough to have his own opinions. On the issue of his parents' divorce he took his mother's side. He knew that the divorce had weakened his father's authority over him, and that it was even further weakened by the settled fact of his own unhappiness and rebellion. It became his policy to do whatever he knew for certain that Marcus didn't want him to do. He was too young to realize that his rebellion against his father became a rebellion against his mother too, and that his taking her side in the divorce had, in the final accounting, only added to her hardships.

And so it came to be that when Virgie would be with his mother on her trips out here at Thanksgiving or Christmas or Easter, he would have his hair in some odd arrangement or color and a ring in his ear and a stud in his nose—I guess to show his father he didn't give a damn, which of course he did or he wouldn't have been trying so hard to act like he didn't.

Once, when Margaret came alone, I asked her, "Is Virgie taking drugs?"

She said, "I don't think so," but, having no gift for deception, she might as well have said yes.

And then Virgie quit coming up here at all. He disappeared, from us and from his mother too.

19
The Branches

Living without expectations is hard but, when you can do it, good. Living without hope is harder, and that is bad. You have got to have hope, and you mustn't shirk it. Love, after all, "hopeth all things." But maybe you must learn, and it is hard learning, not to hope out loud, especially for other people. You must not let your hope turn into expectation.

But whatever you hope, you will find out that you can't bargain with your life on your own terms. It is always going to be proving itself worse or better than you hoped. Whatever we had hoped for Virgie, his absence from us was hard. It was a sorrow. We missed him. We worried about him. In the night, when somebody you need has strayed from you, you worry and you imagine trouble.

Virgie was a long way from knowing how people are bound together. He didn't know, for one thing, how much he was living his mother's life. When he put himself beyond our reach, he put his mother beyond our reach too. The only help she needed, really, was help for him. Because we couldn't help him, we couldn't help her.

We didn't speak of Virgie much, but I knew it was a sorrow to Nathan to have him gone. Virgie had been a big help here by the time he quit helping, when he was sixteen or a little past, and he had been a lot of company. When Virgie disappeared from us he was about eighteen, it was 1994, and Nathan was seventy. At seventy he was still a strong man, well able to work, but he had his aches and pains and he was slowing down.

He was entering into the loneliness that I had seen coming and hoped and prayed against, the loneliness of an old farmer on a farm that seems to be growing old too, because its young people are gone and are not coming back, and there seems less and less reason to keep it going. Nathan was still keeping our place going. He kept the fences and the buildings mended and the roofs painted, but it had been a while since he had made new improvements. The cow herd, by his good judgment, was better than it had ever been, but the sheep and the hogs were long gone, along with the milk cows. The Branches, with Nathan's help when they needed it and he could give it, were raising the crops. We still raised a good garden and kept a few hens.

Things were keeping on in a way, but we and our place were running down. There comes a time in the life of a farm when it needs young people coming on full of strength and hope with the future shining before them. It begins to need work faster than the old people can supply it. Nathan dealt with this by shutting his mouth and going ahead the best he could. And so, mainly, did I.

Life without expectations was still life, and life was still good. The light that had lighted us into this world was lighting us through it. We loved each other and lived right on. We sat down to the food we had grown and ate it and praised it and were thankful for it. We suffered the thoughts of the nights and at dawn woke up and went back to work. The world that so often had disappointed us and made us sorrowful sometimes made us happy by surprise.

You think winter will never end, and then, when you don't expect it, when you have almost forgotten it, warmth comes and a different light. Under the bare trees the wildflowers bloom so thick you can't walk without stepping on them. The pastures turn green and the leaves come.

You look around presently, and it is summer. It has been dry a while, maybe, and now it has rained. The world is so full and abundant it is like a pregnant woman carrying a child in one arm and leading another by the hand. Every puddle in the lane is ringed with sipping butterflies that fly up in a flutter when you walk past in the late morning on your way to get the mail.

And then it is fall and the cornfields are ripe and the calves are fat and shiny and the wooded valley sides are beautiful with color. The sun is bright, the air clear, and the shadows dark. There is the feeling of completion and storing up and getting ready.

You have consented to time and it is winter. The country seems bigger, for you can see through the bare trees. There are times when the woods is absolutely still and quiet. The house holds warmth. A wet snow comes in the night and covers the ground and clings to the trees, making the whole world white. For a while in the morning the world is perfect and beautiful. You think you will never forget.

You think you will never forget any of this, you will remember it always just the way it was. But you can't remember it the way it was. To know it, you have to be living in the presence of it right as it is happening. It can return only by surprise. Speaking of these things tells you that there are no words for them that are equal to them or that can restore them to your mind.

And so you have a life that you are living only now, now and now and now, gone before you can speak of it, and you must be thankful for living day by day, moment by moment, in this presence.

But you have a life too that you remember. It stays with you. You have lived a life in the breath and pulse and living light of the present, and your memories of it, remembered now, are of a different life in a different world and time. When you remember the past, you are not remembering it as it was. You are remembering it as it is. It is a vision or a dream, present with you in the present, alive with you in the only time you are alive.

Your life, as you have lived it, is way back yonder in time. But you are still living, and your living life, expectations subtracted, has a shape, and the shape of it includes the past. The absent and the dead are in it. And the living are in it. As Nathan and I got old and our place called out more and more for younger people, the living who meant the most to us were Danny and Lyda Branch and their children. They had always been part of our membership, we had loved them always, but there came a time when they were necessary to us. We couldn't have got along without them. They have been a godsend.

Danny, as you might say, came into the membership unannounced. Burley was thirty-seven years old when Danny was born. He was surprised, but was well past the time when he might have been greatly astonished that a thing so natural as his long love for Kate Helen Branch should have had a natural result. Before then he had not been a man much excited about results.

And so when Danny made his appearance, the world continued in its daily course without being overly impressed, and so did Burley. Burley knew that certain duties had arrived with his baby son, and he felt the seed of fatherly pride and love sprouting in his heart, but he went on mainly as he had before. He regarded Danny simply as a matter of fact, and without marrying his son's mother, or making any other noticeable change, he simply afforded as much room in his life to Danny as Danny was able to occupy.

The others were not more aware than they had to be that Burley even had a son until Danny appeared in person. He just more or less showed up, following Burley through the woods and fields, Nathan said, like a toy dog on a string, with the smile he was going to be known for already on his face. It was a smile that was going to serve for many words. His eyes were black, as bright as buttons, forever trying to see everything, and not missing much. He would follow Burley for hours, hunting or rambling in the woods, Burley saying almost nothing, Danny nothing at all. Danny grew up with the knowledge of the old economy of the natural world that, for nothing and for pleasure, yielded in its seasons game and fish and nuts and berries and herbs and marketable pelts. "He knows more about all that than he knows he knows," Nathan said, who knew a good deal about it himself and from the same source.

But Danny was a more domestic man than Burley. Burley had had to learn to be domestic, had learned slowly, and had never completely learned. Danny, besides learning early a lot about domestic economy from his mother's housekeeping during the Depression, seemed to have a gift for it. Or you might say that Danny just included the wild world in his domesticity without worrying about the difference. He gathered the woods and the waters into his homelife as a robin gathers mud and straw into her nest. Anyhow, from boyhood he was good at farming and he loved farming, like my Caleb. In his wide-eyed, quiet way he put himself to school to his uncle Jarrat, to Mr. Feltner, to Nathan, to Elton Penn, and to every other good farmer he worked with or could listen to.

That was the education that mattered to him. He stayed in school, because he had to, until he was sixteen. The day he was sixteen, because he no longer had to go, he quit. "What I got out of school," he used to say, "was Lyda."

"And for that," Lyda would answer, "you had better thank the Lord!"

She was right, for she exactly suited him, she was what he needed, and she knew it. She knew too, though she acknowledged it less often and more quietly, that he suited her.

Danny quit school in 1948, the year Nathan and I married. In 1950, after his mother died, Danny married Lyda, when they were still just kids, Danny eighteen and Lyda seventeen, and they moved into the old house with Burley.

I am not sure why, maybe they were just being sensible because they were young and poor, but they didn't have any children for seven years. And then about as fast as it could have been done, they had seven children: Will, Royal, Coulter, Fount, Reuben, Rachel, and Rosie. There were just ten years between Will and Rosie.

Burley took immense pleasure in all this family-making, and he willingly did his share of the work and the watching over. He could be stern enough with the children when he needed to be—"for the sake of survival," Lyda said—but, by preference, he was their playmate or their toy. I have seen them crawling on him like so many pet coons, playing with his hat or his hair, going through his pockets, unfastening his buttons, looking into his ears and nose, feeling his whiskers and his wrinkles.

One day, in the midst of a tumult egged on by Burley, Lyda looked at me and laughed. She said, "Can pleasure have led to *this?*"

And Burley said, "Well, let 'em have a little pleasure of their own."

His pleasure in the children owed a lot, I think, to Lyda and Danny's good sense. The children were allowed to be as rowdy as they pleased as long as they were outdoors. And outdoors they had pretty much the run of the place, along with a regular zoo of cats and dogs, orphan calves and lambs, pet coons and squirrels and groundhogs. They followed the grownups around at work. They played with Danny's tools and whatever was cast off and lying around: old wheels or tires or inner tubes or rope or string or pieces of chain. When they went into the house they were expected to quiet down, "for the sake of survival," and they did. And that didn't mean that they sat in front of the television, either. It meant that they read or played quietly or went to sleep. The older ones helped with the younger ones. They played at work until they were old enough to work, and then they worked. This is what Lyda and Danny expected of them, and this seems to have been what they expected of themselves.

When I think back to the childhood of my own children now, I remember that the thought of their education was always uppermost. Nathan and I, and I more than Nathan, wanted them to go to school. We wanted them to have all the education they needed or wanted, and yet hovering over that thought always was the possibility that once they were educated they would go away, which, as it turned out, they did. We owed them that choice, and we gave it to them, and it might be hard to argue that we were wrong. But I wonder now, and I wonder it many a time, if the other choice, the choice of coming home, might not have been made clearer.

Danny and Lyda's attitude toward education was different from Nathan's and mine. I can see it clearly now. Their attitude maybe had nothing at all to do with the future. The school was there, and so the children went to it. For a while after the oldest ones started, the school was in Port William, and they went there. And then the Port William school was closed, and the children rode down to Hargrave and back every day on the bus. Danny and Lyda seemed not to mind. They just accepted it as it came. They wanted the children to study and learn and behave themselves reasonably well, but I don't think they felt any pressure from the future. I don't think they had the idea that they owed it to the children to send them to college.

When the children got old enough to quit school, if they wanted to quit, they were allowed to do as their father had done. Of the seven, only

Fount, who was the most bookish of the boys, and Rosie finished high school. Every one of them seemed to have a perfect faith in the education they got outside of school, which they didn't even call "education." Out of school, they learned what they evidently thought they needed most to know: to keep house, to raise a garden or a crop, to care for livestock, to break a mule or shoe one, to fix a motor and almost anything else, to hunt, fish, trap, preserve a hide, hive a swarm, cook or preserve anything edible, and to take pleasure in such things. To learn things they didn't know, they asked somebody or they read books. They were a lot like their friends among the Amish.

Compared to nearly everybody else, the Branches have led a sort of futureless life. They have planned and provided as much as they needed to, but they take little thought for the morrow. They aren't going any place, they aren't getting ready to become anything but what they are, and so their lives are not fretful and hankering. And they are all still here, still farming. They are here, and if the world lasts they are going to be here for quite a while. If I had "venture capital" to invest, I think I would invest it in the Branches.

They farm here and on the Feltner place and on the Jarrat Coulter place and on Danny and Lyda's place, which is the Coulter home place, and on another place or two. Royal and Coulter have farms of their own, and so do Rosie and her husband. They survive and go on because they like where they are and what they are doing, they aren't trying to get up in the world, and they produce more than they consume. Except for a manure spreader that Danny bought not long ago from a little Amish factory up in Ohio, I don't think any of them has ever bought a new piece of equipment. A junk yard is a gold mine to them. If horses or mules will work cheaper than a tractor, then they work horses or mules. They use their cisterns and wells, even if the city water line goes right through their front yards. They catch or shoot or find or grow nearly everything they eat. When they need to, they do a little custom work on the side, they trade and contrive and make do, getting by and prospering both at once. It doesn't seem to bother them that while they are making crops and meat and timber, other people are making only money that they sometimes don't even work for.

———

Lyda and I have loved each other for a long time, from the time when she looked up to me as an older woman and teacher to the time when I look up to her as my main prop, my help and comfort. We have done so much sewing together, curtains and clothes and slipcovers and such, that she says we have sewed ourselves together. We have cooked and canned and butchered together and helped our men together.

The number of Lyda's children and children-in-law and grandchildren has grown past her ability to remember birthdays, and she has to keep a list, but she remembers everything else. She knows the history and the goodnesses and the weaknesses of every one of them, and she knows exactly what to get every one of them on their birthdays and at Christmas.

I am in need of presents to give on those days too, of course, but I am a lot less certain of what to get. I usually know pretty well what to get for Margaret, and for a while I knew to a certainty what to get for Virgie. Now I don't know where he is, let alone what he wants or needs. I can guess or suppose with some confidence about Caleb and Alice, but only after I've found something that looks more or less appropriate. About Mattie and his family, who are strangers to me even when they are here, I never have a glimmer. It is tempting to solve that problem by sending money, but I know what that would be. It would be abandonment. And so I always send them *something*.

I need Lyda for that. She is the best present buyer that ever was. Two or three times a year we make a big shopping trip to Louisville. We always take my car, and Lyda drives.

"If you drive, we have got to go in my car," I say. "That makes it fair."

"And a lot more likely that we'll get home," Lyda says, for their vehicles tend to quit regularly at odd times.

We take our lists, and we shop in the malls and talk a lot and eat something unusual and have a splendid time. When I get stumped, Lyda will take on my problem. Sooner or later she will point or hold something up and say, "How about this?" And nine times out of ten it will be just the thing.

Danny gave the same watchful friendliness to Nathan. Heaven will have to pay our debt to them. They have made me glad I have stayed alive, as Burley Coulter used to say.

Part 3

20
The Living

Even old, your husband is the young man you remember now. Even dead, he is the man you remember, not as he was but as he is, alive still in your love. Death is a sort of lens, though I used to think of it as a wall or a shut door. It changes things and makes them clear. Maybe it is the truest way of knowing this dream, this brief and timeless life. Sometimes when I try to remember Nathan, I can't see him exactly enough. Other times, when I haven't thought of him, he comes to me unbidden, and I see him more clearly, I think, than ever I did. Am I awake then, or there, or here?

It is the fall of the year. We have had Thanksgiving. Caleb and Alice were here. And Margaret came, reconciled by now maybe to Virgie's absence, but not one of us spoke of Virgie. I fixed a big dinner, enough to keep us all in leftovers for a while: a young gobbler that Coulter Branch shot and gave to me, dressing and gravy, mashed potatoes, green beans, corn pudding, hot rolls, a cushaw pie. We sat down to it, the four of us, like stray pieces of several puzzles. Nathan would have asked the blessing, and I should have, I tried to, but that turned out to be a silence I could not speak in. I only sat with my head down, while the others waited for me to say something out loud. And then, to change the subject, I said, "Caleb, take a roll and pass 'em."

Soon now it will be Christmas of the two thousandth year of Christ.

Lyda and I have done our shopping. I have wrapped and sent off my gifts to the absent ones, and have nearly finished with the others. I have wrapped Virgie's present and laid it by, in case he reappears. Up in the boys' old room, where the morning light is strong and I do my sewing, I am making new kitchen curtains for Lyda.

I find plenty to do. I keep house and cook. In fit weather I take my walks. For company I go to church or drive over to Lyda and Danny's, or I go and visit an hour or two at Andy and Flora Catlett's to see what is in their minds. Sometimes they drive over here and sit till bedtime. Sometimes, a haunted old woman, I wander about in this house that Nathan and I renewed, that is now aged and worn by our life in it. How many steps, wearing the thresholds? I look at it all again. Sometimes it fills to the brim with sorrow, which signifies the joy that has been here, and the love. It is entirely a gift. There is a silence here now that is the absence of many voices. In that silence I can no longer bear the television or the radio. Margaret and Lyda insist that I keep the telephone, but I hate to hear it ring. I read books, whose voices don't disturb the silence. Sometimes I sit still in my chair late into the night, telling over this story to myself.

I tell it with patience, going over it again and again in order to get it right. Often as my mind moves back and forth over it, I imagine that I am telling it to Andy. That is not hard, for Andy has been listening to me all his life. Andy was in love with me a long time ago, when he was a little boy and I was his uncle's bride. That ended of course. He is not "in love" with me now. He is an aging man with grandchildren. But I know he loves me. He loves us all, the whole membership, living and dead. He has listened to us all, and has stayed with us, farming in his one-handed fashion over there on Harford Run. We are in each other's minds. I perfect these thanks by telling them to him.

As I have told it over, the past visible again in the present, the dead living still in their absence, this dream of time seems to come to rest in eternity. My mind, I think, has started to become, it is close to being, the room of love where the absent are present, the dead are alive, time is eternal, and all the creatures prosperous. The room of love is the love that holds us all, and it is not ours. It goes back before we were born. It goes all the way back. It is Heaven's. Or it is Heaven, and we are in it only by willingness. By whose love, Andy Catlett, do we love this world and ourselves and one another? Do you think we invented it ourselves? I ask with confidence, for I know you know we didn't.

Nathan was sick, and he knew it, he knew it better than I thought he did, a long time before he consented to go to the doctor. He was wearing out, he said, but he wasn't only wearing out, he was sick. He lost weight and strength. He got bony and hollow-cheeked and hollow-eyed. You could see his skull behind his face. He felt bad. He was often almost too ill to get out of bed. But he kept on in his old way, quiet, more pleasant even than usual, staying busy off someplace, mostly by himself.

Margaret and Lyda and I were after him all the time. "Go to the doctor. You have got to go to the doctor."

And Nathan would say, "I'm wearing out. It had to happen, you know." He was not a doctor-going man.

Danny was the only one who did not insist. He just smiled his smile. It wasn't Burley's smile, for there was no sass in it. It was just the smile by which he kept what he knew to himself. I don't think anybody has ever asked Danny, "What are you smiling about?"

Finally we just *made* Nathan go to the doctor. Margaret and I took him to Hargrave. Our doctor there sent him to a specialist in Louisville. The specialist sent him for tests. And so on. Nathan submitted to it all with patience and quietness, even with good humor, knowing, I think, the diagnosis already.

The diagnosis was cancer, dangerously advanced and spreading, inoperable. The doctor spoke to Margaret and me, to avoid looking at Nathan. He went into the technical details, speaking of metastasis and naming organs.

But Nathan was looking at him with a straight, open-eyed look, and the doctor finally felt it. He made himself look back at Nathan, and it was to his credit.

Nathan said, "Say what you mean. It's all right."

"Mr. Coulter," the doctor said, "you are gravely ill, or you soon will be. The prognosis is not good, but without prompt treatment you certainly will not live long."

Without changing his look or his expression, Nathan nodded.

The doctor went on to prescribe an intensive course of therapy, starting with radiation. It was a story we all knew, one that has been lived and told too many times in Port William, a bad story.

But I was surprised when Nathan, without exactly interrupting, stood up. He had come to the end of his submission, though not of his patience or his quietness. He put out his hand, which the doctor a little wonderingly shook. Nathan said, "Thank you, doctor. Thank you for all you've done."

He went out, and Margaret and I, having no choice, followed.

I knew then what he had been doing. For a good while after he got sick, he thought he would just work it off the way he always had, he would get well. And then the truth came to him, and he faced it. After that, he was loitering, putting us off, giving himself a chance to be captured by his death before he could be captured by the doctors and the hospitals and the treatments and the tests and the rest of it. When he consented to go to the doctor he was only consenting for the rest of us to be told what he already knew. He was dying.

We parted with Margaret, who had met us at the doctor's office. We went home. Nathan hung up his suit, which he would not wear again alive, and got back into his work clothes. He walked up to the barn, and I heard him start the tractor. He put out hay for the cows. It was February, they would be calving soon, and I knew he would look at every one of them. He did his other chores. He filled the woodbox on the back porch. He built up the fires for the evening. And then he sat down in his chair by the stove in the kitchen and picked up the newspaper.

I was working at the counter by the sink, not daring to turn around. I was brokenhearted, furious, scared, and confused, crying, and determined not to let him see that I was. I was beating the hell out of a dozen egg whites in a bowl. Why I had started making a cake, I don't know. It was what my hands had found to do, and I was doing it.

And was Nathan sitting over there actually reading the paper? Well, I knew he was holding it up and looking at it. For all I know, he may have been reading it. But I knew too that he was thinking of me. My steadfast comfort for fifty years and more had been to know that I was on his mind. Whatever was happening between us, I knew I was on his mind, and that was where I wanted to be. He was thinking of me, I was sure of that, but he had got ahead of me too. He had dealt with what the doctor had told us even before he had gone to the doctor. And now, in a way too late, I was having to deal with it. Looking back, I can see there was something ridiculous about it. There we were at a great crisis in our lives, and it had to be, it could only be, dealt with as an ordinary thing. Nathan had seen that. For my sake as much as his own, he was insisting on it. But I was too upset to see it then.

My tears were falling into the bowl of beaten eggs and then my nose dripped into it. I flung the whole frothy mess into the sink. I said, "Well, what are you planning to do? Just die? Or what?"

I couldn't turn around. I heard him fold the paper. After a minute he said, "Dear Hannah, I'm going to live right on. Dying is none of my business. Dying will have to take care of itself."

He came to me then, an old man weakened and ill, with my Nathan looking out of his eyes. He held me a long time as if under a passing storm, and then the quiet came. I fixed some supper, and we ate.

He lived right on.

The next morning after breakfast, with the sunlight pouring in through the kitchen windows, we sat on at the table a long time, talking of a number of things, practical things. We set our life before us as it was, and set ourselves before our life as we were, talking of what needed to be done, as we had talked many times.

And then Nathan changed the tune. Looking straight at me, much as he had looked at the doctor the day before, and taking up that subject again, he said, "I have had a good life, especially the part you know. I have liked it and am thankful for it. I don't want to end up as a carcass for a bunch of carrion crows, each one taking his piece, and nobody in charge. I don't want to be worn all to holes like an old shirt no good for rags."

I understood him. He wanted to die at home. He didn't want to be going someplace all the time for the sake of a hopeless hope. He wanted to die as himself out of his own life. He didn't want his death to be the end of a technological process. I nodded.

He said, "I'm asking this of you, Hannah. I know it's a lot to ask. I'm sorry."

I said, "It's not what you're asking of me that I'm sorry for. And you don't have to be sorry. Do you remember what we promised?"

"Yes," he said. "I remember."

As the opportunities came, I talked with Margaret and Lyda. We tried to foresee needs and make plans. We went back, the three of us, to our doctor down at Hargrave.

"He doesn't want to die of a cure," I said.

The doctor didn't want to comment on that. He nodded.

I said, "I expect there will be pain." There was already pain, as I knew, but Nathan had not said so, and so I did not.

"There will be pain," the doctor said.

"Will you help us to deal with that?" Margaret asked him.

The doctor nodded. "I will help you deal with that."

"We're talking about medicine," Lyda said. "Dope."

The doctor smiled and nodded again. "Yes. I will help with that." And he wrote out a prescription and handed it to me.

"So you'll have it when he needs it."

Living right on called for nothing out of the ordinary. We made no changes. We only accepted the changes as they came. Margaret came out more often than before, but she made her visits casual and not too long. Caleb came when he could. And Danny, I noticed, began showing up every day, maybe not stopping by the house, maybe not seeing Nathan, but keeping an eye on us, watching for what needed to be done and trying to get it done before it could worry Nathan. The spring work was beginning, and so Danny always had reasons to come or to send one of the boys.

Nathan knew we had pain medicine, and the time came when he needed to ask for it, but usually he would take it only at night. He didn't like what it did to his mind. It made him feel wrong. He went on as he was able, going about the place and his work, giving it up only as he had to. As he gave it up, Danny quietly took it on.

One day, sort of laughing, he said, "Hannah, I'd go to the barn and see to things, but I'm afraid if I got there I couldn't get back."

It was April by then, a sunny morning and warm out. I said, "Well, why don't you go out on the porch and sit a while in the sun?" He went out, and I called Danny to come and see to things at the barn.

The time soon came when he could not get out of bed. Lyda or Danny began staying at night during the week, Margaret on the weekends. And still Nathan would take the pain medicine only at night. He lay there in the daytime lucidly suffering.

Way in the night I heard him stir and cry out, not loudly. I got up to see about him.

I said, "Do you need anything?"

"No," he said.

"Are you all right?"

"Yes."

But I sat down in a chair by the bed. The house got altogether still again, and I thought he was asleep. Just ever so quietly I reached over and laid my hand on his shoulder.

He said, "I love you too, Hannah."

He didn't last long after that. Death had become his friend. They say that people, if they want to, can let themselves slip away when the time comes. I think that is what Nathan did. He was not false or greedy. When the time came to go, he went.

Lyda and Andy Catlett and I were with him when he died. It was about suppertime, still daylight, the sun and the wind in the perfect new maple leaves outside the window. A dove called, somewhere off toward town a screen door slammed, and he was gone.

After the stillness had come and was complete, I telephoned Margaret. She was here in just over an hour with her suitcase packed. She had been expecting the call. Caleb was here early the next morning, having given up on sleep sometime before midnight and come on, leaving Alice to come the next day. He was quiet, steady, helpful, sweet as always, and, I could tell, grieved to the bone.

It was still the middle of the afternoon, office hours, on the West Coast when I called Mattie. I couldn't get any living human at his office, and so I left a message on his recording machine: "Mattie, this is your momma. Your dad died a while ago. Call me up."

He called back in about an hour. He wanted to come home, he said, he would give anything to be here. But he was too much involved right then in things that depended on him, that he just couldn't get out of. In fact, he was shortly to leave on a trip to China for a meeting with business people there, an opportunity that might not come again. He was giving me the picture of a man snarled in a tangle, helpless to get free.

I knew that he didn't have the strength to get free. His life was being driven by a kind of flywheel. He had submitted to it and accepted it. It was turning fast. To slow it down or stop it and come to a place that was moving with the motion only of time and loss and slow grief was more, that day, than he could imagine.

I knew too that it was more than he could bear. He is in a way given over to machines, but he is not a machine himself. Right then, he could not bear the thought of coming back to stand even for a few hours by his dead father in the emptiness he once had filled. He said he would come as soon as he could.

There was a time when Port William drew its members into itself every Saturday night to shop, trade, talk, court, play, argue, loaf, or whatever else they had to be together in order to do. Now Port William, or what is left of it, is most likely to assemble, not in Port William at all, but in the Tacker Funeral Home in Hargrave. The survivors of the old life come to pay their respects. The neighbors, old and young, come. People who have moved away, maybe a long time ago, come back. You see people you knew when you were young and now don't recognize, people who may never come back again, people you may never see again. We feel the old fabric torn, pulling apart, and we know how much we have loved each other.

I greeted them all, standing by Nathan's coffin, with Margaret, Caleb and Alice, Lyda and Danny, the Catlett brothers and their wives standing with me or always somewhere near. The kin and the friends and the neighbors filed past. I took their hands, received their hugs, their smiles, their kind tears, their words of comfort:

"I'm sorry, Hannah."

"Sorry, Miz Coulter."

"We love you both."

"There won't be another one like him."

"Anything you need, you let us know."

"We'll miss him."

"I'm sorry."

"He was one of the old good ones."

"One of them things."

And they would pass along to gather in bunches, standing or sitting, in the other rooms, talking, remembering, laughing, as they always do.

I had been a grieving girl once, and now I was a grieving old woman. I knew how I wanted to appear, and I required myself to appear that way: an old woman whose grief might be supposed but was little to be seen, who was fully capable and in charge, helpful to other grievers, above all useful to herself. The death of an old man is not the same as the death of a young one. It is not wrong, it is not a surprise. It has been a long time coming. You have seen it coming a long time. You know in your own heart what it means, but you must not ask too much of other people.

And then there was the funeral. The sixth of May. Eleven o'clock in the morning. Not twenty minutes beforehand, Mattie came. He was standing by the coffin, flustered and shaken, everybody looking at him, before I recognized him and could believe it was him. He had flown to Cincinnati, rented a car, dashed down the interstate, and made it barely in time. And he had to hurry back one breath after the preacher said the final amen. I had to think of all it had cost, of all the engines that had run, just to give one man a few minutes of ordinary grief at his dad's funeral, but I was completely glad to see him. I sat between him and Caleb during the service; it was as it should have been. And then there was the return to Port William, and the brief words and the parting at the grave.

The kitchen at home was full of brought-in food. It is wonderful how much grief and sympathy in Port William have gone into cooking. Tables were spread and prepared. Everybody who wanted to come came and ate, a lot of people, a lot of commotion and talk. When they had eaten and visited and again spoken their kindnesses, the company scattered, went back to their cars in the yard and the barn lot, and drove off. Mattie was long gone by then, on his way to China, I suppose. Caleb and

Alice had a long drive, and I shooed them off. The neighbor women who had come in to lay out the food and do the kitchen work finished up and left. Margaret and Lyda helped me to set the house to rights. Lyda hugged me then and went home, taking food for supper.

Margaret said, "Momma, can't I stay with you a few days? I would like to."

I said, "No, Margaret. I want you to go. Go home and do the things you need to do. I'm all right."

I was telling the truth. I was all right. I was going to live right on.

After she left, the house slowly filled up with silence. Nathan's absence came into it and filled it. I suffered my hard joy, I gave my thanks, I cried my cry. And then I turned again to that other world I had taught myself to know, the world that is neither past nor to come, the present world where we are alive together and love keeps us.

21
Okinawa

I married the war twice, as you might say, once in ignorance, once in knowledge. And yet I knew of it only what we suffered of it at home and what I read of it in the newspaper at the time, and later the little I sometimes saw of it on television. But of the actual experience of actual people in the war, I knew little. Of what Nathan had actually known and done and suffered in the fighting on Okinawa, I knew nothing.

That is maybe not so hard to understand. Our life from the day we married until Nathan died was like a stretched strand. We had our obligations to meet and our work to do, the tasks overlapped and kept on, before the work of one year had ended the work of the next year began. I don't think Nathan himself dwelled more on the war than he had to, but I think he had to dwell on it. I think he saw the war as in a way the circumstance of the rest of his life. I know he dreamed about it. I know he did not talk about it.

He did not talk about it, I understood, because it was painful to remember, and for the same reason I did not ask him about it. Now that I have taken the pains to learn something about it, I had better ask if I really wanted to know. I did. I needed to know, but I am not glad to know.

I learned enough to know why I didn't learn it any sooner. Nathan was not the only one who was in it, who survived it and came home from it, and did not talk about it. There were several from Port William who went and fought and came home and lived to be old men here, whose memories contained in silence the farthest distances of the world, terrible sights, terrible sufferings. Some of them were heroes. And they said not a word. They stood among us like monuments without inscriptions. They said nothing or said little because we have barely a language for what they knew, and they could not bear the pain of talking of their knowledge in even so poor a language as we have.

They knew the torment of the whole world at war, that nobody could make or end or escape alone, in which everybody suffered alone. As many who have known it have said of it, war is Hell. It is the outer darkness beyond the reach of love, where people who do not know one another kill one another and there is weeping and gnashing of teeth, where nothing is allowed to be real enough to be spared.

Hell is a shameful place, and it is hard to speak of what you know of it. It is hard to live in Port William and yet have in mind the blasted and burnt, bloodied and muddy and stinking battlegrounds of Okinawa, hard to live in one place and imagine another. It is hard to live one life and imagine another. But imagination is what is needed. Want of imagination makes things unreal enough to be destroyed. By imagination I mean knowledge and love. I mean compassion. People of power kill children, the old send the young to die, because they have no imagination. They have power. Can you have power and imagination at the same time? Can you kill people you don't know and have compassion for them at the same time?

I was changed by Nathan's death, because I had to be. Our life together here was over. It was my life alone that had to go on. The strand had slackened. I had begun the half-a-life you have when you have a whole life that you can only remember. I began this practice of sitting sometimes long hours into the night, telling over this story, this life, that even when it was only mine was wholly Nathan's and mine because for the term of this world we were wholly each other's. We were each other's chance to live in the room of love where we could be known well enough to be spared. We were each other's gift.

But in my telling I pretty soon had to reckon with Nathan's silence about the war. Out of all I knew of him came this need to know what he had known that I did not know. I went to the library and found books. I found some imperfect and false books, some picture books, for instance, that showed only the enemy dead. And I found some that were true, terrible for being true, brave enough to be terrible enough to be true. I didn't find out what happened to Nathan himself, of course, for what he knew will not be known again. I found out the sort of thing you would have known if you were a soldier and were there on Okinawa in the spring of 1945 when Easter and the beginning of battle both came on April Fool's Day.

You went from an ordinary day in the ordinary world into the world of war, an exploding world where you lived inescapably hour after hour, day after day, killing as you were bidden to do, suffering as you were bidden to do, dying as you were bidden to do. You were there to kill until you were killed. And this would finally seem to be the only world there was.

It was a world where no place was safe, where you or your friends could be killed in any place at any minute.

You were living, it seemed, inside a dark cloud filled with lightning and thunder: thousands of tons of explosives, bombs and shells, machine gun and rifle fire. The air was full of death. In some units, sooner or later, everybody was hit.

You see a friend, shot and dying, lying in the dirt. A medical corpsman is kneeling beside him, tenderly touching his face, making the sign of the cross over him, weeping.

Mortar shells are coming in as you open a can of food and try to eat. The friend beside you is hit, his head blown off. His brains spatter your clothes and your food. You start to vomit, and you cannot stop.

You are standing beside your friend. A shell comes in and explodes. Your friend, knocked down, attempts to leap up and discovers that he has no legs. He dies. You cannot forget this.

You have killed your enemy. You have seen his face as he died, the face of a living young man dying. You cannot forget this. Compassion makes the suffering worse. In the world of war everything makes everything worse.

Death falls from the sky. It flies in the air. The ground fills with the dead. The rain falls day after day. Mud makes everything worse. It is harder to bring up supplies, harder to move, harder to bring out the wounded and to bury the dead.

Under fire, you attempt to dig a foxhole, and you dig right into the body of a man, rotten and full of maggots.

The dead are blasted out of their graves. If you slip on a muddy slope and fall, you get up covered with maggots. They are on your clothes, on your skin, in your pockets.

Flies are everywhere. Recalling the words of politicians about gallantry and sacrifice, one survivor said, "Only the flies benefited." The flies spread dysentery. You are wet, muddy, soiled with your own shit, and you live day after day, night after night in the same clothes.

The battlefield stinks of rotting flesh, excrement, vomit, the smoke of explosives and of everything that will burn.

Because of the stench and the noise and the never-ending fear, your rations, which are never appetizing, become harder and harder to eat. You are exhausted, and you cannot rest. As the weeks go by, you lose weight, maybe twenty pounds. You know, from looking at your friends, that you no longer look like yourself.

It goes on without mercy, the fear unending, worst at night. At night the quiet sounds worry you most. At night you never know the origin of a quiet sound. Is it a friend or an enemy? Are you hearing things? Are you losing your mind? You have to make up your mind that you will not lose your mind.

You find where the enemy buried one of theirs, leaving a green branch in his canteen on his grave. Compassion makes it worse.

You performed the cruelties that were required and sometimes cruelties that were not, and what would your folks have thought?

You fought for days without knowing where you were, when the known world consisted of what you could see, the few friends fighting on either side of you, and the unknown enemy in front. You were lost in an enormous fact. The ones of you who were lost in it may never quite have found your way out of it, and nobody outside it would ever quite understand it. How far from home were you? How far beyond the political slogans? You were one of an army of young men fighting to stay alive, and you were fighting an army of young men who finally were fighting only to die. They had to be killed, almost every one of them.

You knew the terrible loneliness of the thought that your life was worth nothing. You were expendable. You were being spent. Your folks could not have imagined what you were going through, you could not want them to know, you would never tell them.

What saved it from utter meaninglessness and madness and ruin was the love between you and your friends fighting beside you. For them, you did what you had to do to try to stay alive, to try to keep them alive. For them, you did heroic acts that you did not know were heroic.

What saved it were the medical corpsmen and stretcher-bearers who went out again and again into the fields of fire to bring away the wounded, who brought something angelic into that Hell of misery and hurt and destruction and death.

What saved it was the enormous pity that seemed to accumulate in the air over it.

To read of that battle when you love a man who was in it, that is hard going. I read in wonder, believing and sickened. I read weeping. Because I didn't know exactly what had happened to Nathan, it *all* seemed to have happened to him.

You can't give yourself over to love for somebody without giving yourself over to suffering. You can't give yourself to love for a soldier without giving yourself to his suffering in war. It is this body of our suffering that Christ was born into, to suffer it Himself and to fill it with light, so that beyond the suffering we can imagine Easter morning and the peace of God on little earthly homelands such as Port William and the farming villages of Okinawa.

But Christ's living unto death in this body of our suffering did not end the suffering. He asked us to end it, but we have not ended it. We suffer the old suffering over and over again. Eventually, in loving, you see that you have given yourself over to the knowledge of suffering in a state of war that is always going on. And you wake in the night to the thought of the hurt and the helpless, the scorned and the cheated, the burnt, the bombed, the shot, the imprisoned, the beaten, the tortured, the maimed, the spit upon, the shit upon.

The Battle of Okinawa was not a battle only of two armies making war against each other. It was a battle of both armies making war against a place and its people.

Before that spring, Okinawa had been a place of ancient country villages and farming landscapes of little fields, perfectly cultivated. The people were poor by our standards now but peaceable and courteous, hospitable and kind. They hated violence and had no weapons. They made music and sang when they rested from their work in the fields. It was "a land of song and dance." The people made beautiful things with their hands: buildings and gardens, weaving and pottery. They had survived conquest, poverty, storms and drouths, disease and hunger, but they had met no calamity like the battle of 1945. It killed 150,000 of them as the fighting drove them out of their homes and they wandered with their children and old people into the fields of fire. They were killed by mistake. Nobody intended to kill them, they were just in the wrong place. It was their own place, but the war had made it wrong.

And their beloved, lovely island was scoured and burned. Everything standing was destroyed: houses, trees, gardens, tombs, towns, the capital city of Naha, the beautiful castle of Shuri. I found books with photographs of beautiful buildings, walls and gates, bridges and gardens, all "destroyed in 1945." I found a photograph of some tanks driving across little fields, leaving deep tracks.

I began to imagine something I know I cannot actually imagine: a human storm of explosions and quakes and fire, a man-made natural disaster gathering itself up over a long time out of ignorance and hatred, greed and pride, selfishness and a silly love of power. I imagined it gathering up into armies of "ignorant boys, killing each other" and passing like a wind-driven fire over the quiet land and kind people. I knew then what Nathan knew all his life: It can happen anywhere.

Like any storm, it finally ended. Like any fire, it burnt itself out. Like all the living, those doomed to die finally were dead. I imagined the quiet coming again over the burnt and blasted land. I imagined a green slope somewhere undestroyed where a fresh, untainted breeze blew in from the sea. I imagined Nathan coming there alone and sitting down, facing home, knowing that he had lived and would live, the quiet coming over him, rest coming to him. And I imagined Port William, the town, the farmsteads, the fields and the woods, the river valley and the long, slow river, taking shape again in his mind.

And so I came to know, as I had not known before, what this place of ours had been and meant to him. I knew, as I had not known before, what I had meant to him. Our life in our place had been a benediction to him, but he had seen it always within a circle of fire that might have closed upon it.

He was a rock to me, but now I knew that he had been shaken. Okinawa shook him, and he was shaken for life, and deep in the night he needed to touch me. I didn't know the reason then, but now I know that some old nightmare of the war had come back to him and frightened him awake. And ever so quietly, ever so gently, so as not to wake me, he would touch me. I would pretend to sleep on, so as not to disturb him with the thought that he had wakened me. It was not a lover's touch. As I knew partly then but know completely now, he needed to know that he was here and I was here with him, that he had come from the world of war, again, to this. Reassured, he would sleep again, and I too would sleep.

Now I remember, now I seem to dream again, that sleep of ours, helpless and dark, precious and brief, somehow allowed within the encircling fire.

22

Next?

After Nathan died, my Margaret or Lyda Branch, wanting I suppose to divert my mind, would offer me "a change of scenery."

"Would you like to go for a drive?"

"No," I would say, "I don't think so."

I have my regular ways of going where I need to go, and I stick to them. There are a lot of places I don't go back to now.

There was a time when Nathan and I would enjoy going for a little drive just in the neighborhood, maybe late in the evening of a hot day, to cool off and see how everybody's crops were doing. Every farm then was farmed by people we knew. But now too many of the old families have died out or gone. Farms have been divided or gathered into bigger farms; or they have been bought by people in the cities who need a place to "get away," and who visit them for a while and then lose interest and sell them again. Such things I would just as soon not see.

A decent half a year, about, after Nathan died, Kelly Crowley paid me a visit. I heard a car stop, went to the back door to see who it was, and it was Kelly. Here he came across the backyard, a big man, nodding and smiling and waving, his big diamond ring flashing on his big hand, his big car shining behind him.

"Kelly Crowley!" I said. "How long has it been since I saw you? Come in here and tell me how you are."

I already had a good idea why he had come, I am sorry to say, but I was glad to see him, even so. Kelly was raised in Port William. He is the same age as my Caleb, they were schoolmates. I held him in my lap when he was little. He came here to play many a time. I have fed him many a meal. He was a rather chubby boy, almost dainty in the way he walked and used his hands. He suffered a good deal of mistreatment from the other boys, which he didn't deserve then but by now has probably managed to deserve. They called him, of course, "Killer Crawley." After high school, he moved to Hargrave, learned the real estate business, and has done, as they say, well. He has an expensive house, an expensive car, a wife and three children, each of whom has an expensive car, and none of whom would recognize as Kelly the boy I used to know, who had nothing except a bad start as the stepson of a poor tenant farmer and maybe the sweetest smile in the world, which maybe more or less in spite of himself he still means.

The interstate highway that transformed everything within its reach also transformed Kelly Crowley. Along the widened road from the interstate to Hargrave there is the same ugly splatter of motels, filling stations, fastfood places, liquor stores, and shopping centers that you will find everywhere else, and that is Kelly's theater of operations. That, and commuter housing developments with views, transformed Kelly from a livestock trader, auctioneer, and real estate dealer into a "developer" and a wealthy man with his thumb in the political pie. It is also the source of the extreme anxiety that those who know him well can see behind his smile. Kelly is dogged by the suspicion that other people know things he does not know, that profitable deals are being made without his knowledge, that desirable properties are being made available at a low price to somebody else. He has spent his life learning what other people have, how they got it, what they paid for it, what it is now worth, and how to get it. By something in his manner he seems always to be referring to the self-denial and the sacrifice that he has had to suffer in making himself rich. He is a martyr to his own wealth and importance.

And yet his smile is as sweet as it was when he was a boy. His manners are as winning as ever. In his absence you tell yourself you would just as soon not see him again, and then he shows up and you are glad to see him.

"Come in," I said. I held the door open for him. "Sit down there at the table. Let me fix you a cup of coffee."

He came in. He gave me a little bow, smiling. He said, "Yes, mam, Mrs. Coulter, I will allow you to do that, if you please."

He sat down. "Mrs. Coulter, I was surely sorry to hear about Mr. Coulter's passing. I wasn't at home at the time or you surely would have seen me. I was away on a little trip, the wife and I."

What do you say? I said, "Thank you, Kelly."

"And how are the children? Caleb, I imagine, doing fine?"

"They're all doing fine," I said.

"Well!" Kelly said. That is his word when an exclamation of friendship and concern seems to be called for. It could mean approval or disapproval, or almost anything else. Sometimes it means he is not listening.

"Caleb is still doing his research and writing his articles. He and Alice are fine."

"Well!"

"Margaret is still teaching school."

"Well!"

"And Mattie is in China or someplace, I reckon. He's always someplace else."

"Well!"

When it was ready, I brought cups of coffee for us both, gave him his, and sat down with mine.

He gave me a bow and a smile, and thanked me. "Well, I'm glad to hear they're all doing well. Mighty glad." He put in cream and sugar. He stirred rapidly and delicately.

"And how are you, Mrs. Coulter?" he said, smiling and bowing. "In good health, I imagine, as always?"

He was looking straight at me through his smile, making his own diagnosis, and I was moved to look straight back. "Just fine," I said.

"Well, I just imagine you maybe might be moving down to Louisville to live with Margaret one of these days?"

I was ready for that, but I let the remark hang in the air for a while to get the full benefit of it. It managed to be all at the same time a question, a recommendation, and an expression of sympathy for an old widow living alone. He finished stirring, laid the spoon down, picked up his cup with his little finger extended, and bestowed a tiny kiss upon the rim.

I said, "No." And that hung in the air a while, sounding short. Just in time, I remembered Mrs. Feltner, who would have been nice to the Devil himself, on the chance that he might improve if treated well. "No, Kelly," I said. "I haven't thought of that. I've made no plans of that kind."

"Well! Surely, Mrs. Coulter, you aren't thinking of living on here by yourself?"

"I am thinking of living right on, right here."

"By yourself? I just made sure you'd be going to live with Margaret or some of 'em."

"I'm still capable of looking after myself," I said. "And of course I am looked after."

"Well! Oh, I imagine! I imagine Danny Branch and them will be farming your place for you?"

"Yes, I'll always be able to depend on Danny."

"Oh, they don't make 'em no finer than Danny Branch. No, *mam!*" He was drinking his coffee in something of a hurry, but precisely, in little sips. "You have a nice place here, Mrs. Coulter." He said this looking swiftly around at the kitchen, into the living room, out the back window at the barn and the ridge rising behind it, inventorying and appraising everything. After such a look, I believe he could have gone back to his office and made a long list. "A *lovely* place."

I said, "A lot of work and love has gone into the keeping of it."

He spoke then under the obligation and burden of old friendship, a man of his authority being unable to stand by at such a time and *not* speak: "Have you given any thought to the final disposition of it?"

By then, behind his smile and his big, dainty hands, I could see his anxiety, his almost panic. He was assuming, as I knew from the start, that as an old widow woman I would not know what I had or the worth of it, that I might not live long, that if I died and the children inherited the place, they *would* know the worth of it. They, being less provincial and backward than I am, would be harder to deal with than I would be.

"Yes," I said. And then I said something that I had not thought of before, but have hardly ceased to think of since: "I am giving some thought to putting it into a land trust, to keep it from ever being developed."

"Well!" he said.

"And I have given some thought to donating it as a wildlife preserve."

"Well!"

"And I have thought of having myself buried right in the narrowest part of the lane, with a stout rock wall around my grave."

"Well!" he said, as if this was just the sort of thing that nice old ladies like me usually did.

He had finished his coffee. I stood up, and then he did. He took out his wallet and laid his business card on the table as he might have laid down a tip. "Well, Mrs. Coulter," he said, as if the previous things had never been uttered, "if you ever decide to sell, I surely would be obliged if you'd give me a chance to talk with you."

"Of course, Kelly! I'll always be glad of a chance to talk with you."

And then, the Devil getting his work accomplished in spite of me, I heard myself say, "Kelly, I see you're putting on a lot of weight. I want you to take care of yourself. I'm busy here every day, and I would hate to have to quit and go to a funeral."

He couldn't think what to say. The idea of an old widow with desirable property sitting alive at his funeral turned his world of real estate upside down like a salt shaker, and shook it. He gave me a quick unsmiling look, said "Yes, mam," and smiled.

We parted at the kitchen door with expressions of mutual affection, perhaps real enough.

But my world had got shaken too. The sound of his engine had hardly died away before I realized that I could no longer imagine our place, I couldn't see it in my mind's eye. What did *he* see in it? A "country place" for some rich professional person in Louisville or Cincinnati, with our old once-renewed buildings shoved into a heap and burnt and everything brand-new? A hunting preserve for some sportsman's club? A housing development called "The Woodlands"? Whatever vision he had of the place as it might be had driven the place as it is out of my mind. I felt bereft, and a little crazy. I felt a fierce homesickness. I put on my scarf and coat and went out.

Of course, there it all was, familiar of old, just as I knew it, the shape of it clear and clean in the late fall with the trees bare, the wind brisk and cool, the cattle lying down in the sun up on the ridge. I walked up among them to where I could see across the Feltner place to the roofs and gables and the church steeple of Port William, with the fields and fencerows and woodlands lying about it. It had been my homeland in this world nearly sixty years, the homeland that Virgil had died from in his absence and never seen again, that Nathan had remembered and cherished in his mind and come back to.

It was as familiar as my old headscarf and coat and shoes, as my body. I have lived from it all these years. When I am buried in it at last my flesh will be the same as it, and hardly a difference made. But I have seen it change. It has changed, it is changing, and it is threatened.

The old neighborliness has about gone from it now. The old harvest crews and their talk and laughter at kitchen tables loaded with food have been replaced by machines, and by migrant laborers who eat at the store. The old thrift that once kept us alive has been replaced by extravagance and waste. People are living as if they think they are in a movie. They are all looking in one direction, toward "a better place," and what they see is no thicker than a screen. The houses in Port William and even on some of the farms are more and more being used as temporary lodgings by people who temporarily, as they think, can do no better. Port William is becoming a sort of whatnot shelf where, until they can find "a better place," people live and move and have their being.

The old Port William that I came to in 1941 I think of now as a sort of picture puzzle. It was not an altogether satisfactory picture. It always required some forgiveness, for things that of course could be forgiven. But the picture was more or less complete and more or less put together, and the pieces were more or less replaceable. After the war ended in 1945, slowly at first but ever faster, the lost pieces were not replaced. Sometimes, as when we buried the old Feltners or Mr. Milo Settle, the new grave contained a necessary and forever finished part of the old life. The new life seems to be composed of pieces of several different puzzles never to be completed. And who is to blame for this? I don't know. Whoever caused it, it is everybody's disease, and nobody could have caused it who didn't have it.

Like a lot of old people I have known, I am now living in two places: the place as it was and the place as it is. As it was it is almost always present to me, with the dead moving about in it as they were: Virgil, Old Jack Beechum, Mat and Margaret Feltner, Joe and Nettie Banion, Burley and Jarrat Coulter, Art and Mart Rowanberry, Elton and Mary Penn, Bess and Wheeler Catlett, Nathan. By the ones who have moved away, as many have done, as my children have done, the dead may be easily forgotten. But to those who remain, the place is always forever a reminder. And so the absent come into presence.

I knew as I walked about that day after Kelly's visit that I will do whatever I can to see that this place is not desecrated after I am dead. But I am not going to have myself buried in the lane. I will be buried up on the hill at Port William beside Nathan, to wait for the Resurrection with him and the others.

I walked down off the ridge into the woods farthest from the road. I found the path where the slope is not too steep. The sun was bright, and under the brow of the hill I was out of the wind. I was idling along with my stick, recognizing the trees and wishing them well.

And then I saw this hunter slipping along through the undergrowth slowly and quietly, coming more or less toward me. He was wearing camouflage clothes, but I saw him a good while before he saw me. I let him get close, and then I said, "Good afternoon, young man."

He took a step backward and said "Oh!" And then he pretended not to be surprised. He said, "Hello! Are you Mrs. Coulter?"

I said, "No."

"Well," he said, "we have Mrs. Coulter's permission to hunt here."

"We who?"

"Me and my buddy."

"I suppose you do," I said. "She's a generous old woman."

23

Virge

Now we are in the new year of 2001, also a new century, also a new millennium, and it is the same world still. Here in Port William, it seems, we are waiting. For what? For the last of the old rememberers and the old memories to disappear forever? For the coming of knowledge that will make us a community again? For the catastrophe that will force us to become a community again? For the catastrophe that will end everything? For the Second Coming? The only thing at all remarkable that has happened is that Virgie has come back.

It was a quiet evening about the first of February. I had started fixing myself a bite of supper. When I heard a rather noisy old car come in and stop behind the house, I thought it must be some of the Branches. They operate a fleet of junkers, and I can't tell which is which by the sounds they make. But I didn't hear a car door shut and nobody came to the kitchen door, so I went out to see.

It was getting on toward dark, but I could see the car well enough, and I didn't recognize it. I hesitated a minute. The country is full of strangers now, and you hear tales. There are, no doubt about it, some people who would knock an old woman in the head more or less on speculation. But I thought "What of it?" and went on out.

The driver of the car had just stopped and leaned forward onto the steering wheel. I could see a head of beautiful long hair and I thought at first it was a woman, but when I got closer I saw it was a man. I rapped on the window and he raised his head.

It was Virgie. He looked like death warmed over, and his face was wet with tears. He looked like a man who had been lost at sea and had made it to shore at last, but had barely made it. I could feel the ghosts gathering round as they had done at his mother's wedding. Time was when I too would have wept at that homecoming, but though a big ache of love passed through my heart, I shed no tears. I don't think I am going to weep anymore.

But he was weeping, with relief, I think, and sorrow and regret. Maybe it was some feeling of unworthiness that kept him from moving. Maybe he had given himself permission to come back, but he couldn't give himself permission to get out of the car.

I rapped on the window again, and he rolled it down. I said, "Virgie, come on to the house, honey, and let me fix you some supper."

I went back to the house myself then, and he got out and followed me. He hesitated at the door, and I said, "Come in."

He came in and shut the door. I said, "Go in yonder and wash." He did. He minded like a good child. He had not said a word. I set about finding something to cook. He finished up in the bathroom and came back to the kitchen, walking as soundlessly as a cat. I realized that he was making his way through a series of permissions that I would have to give. He needed permission to be there as himself, as my grandson, as before. He needed permission to be there in Nathan's absence. He needed, maybe, permission to live. He had pulled his hair back and tied it.

I said, "Does your mother know where you are?"

"No," he said. His first word.

I said, "Then go call her up and tell her." He started into the living room to the telephone. I said, "And tell her you love her. I imagine she needs to know."

I heard him talking. I don't know what he said. He was in there a good while.

When he came back I had supper on the table. I said, "Sit down."

He sat down and I filled his plate. I said, "Eat."

He was gaunt and hollow-cheeked and had an unsure look in his eyes. He ate a lot.

When we had eaten, I said, "Well, what brings you back?"

He started to say "You," and couldn't, and said, "This."

I said, "This?"

He said, "I want to be here. I want to live here and farm. It's the only thing I really want to do. I found that out."

I said, "Maybe you can do that. You have still got it to do. We can see. There's nothing to stop you from trying."

He said, "Thank you. I would like to try."

I said, "Do you have stuff you need to bring in?"

When he came in with it, I said, "There's a clean towel and washrag for you if you want a bath. I'm going up now to fix your bed."

I made his bed for him in his old room and came down and busied myself in the kitchen. He took his bath and I heard him go up the stairs. When I knew he was in bed, I went up and gave a little knock on his door and went in. I leaned over him and gave him a kiss. I said, "Are you going to be warm enough? Do you have enough covers?"

"Yes," he said. "Thank you."

I said, "Sleep tight."

That was a month ago. The next day I handed him over to Danny Branch.

Danny happened to stop by the house early that morning to call for Reuben or one of Reuben's boys to come and help him with a calving heifer. I was just starting to fix breakfast. I had heard Virgie up and stirring about, but I knew he would not come down until I called him. There were a lot of permissions yet to be given.

When Danny had made his call and come back into the kitchen, I said, "Danny, can you use another hand?"

"Who?"

"Virgie."

"*Virgie?*"

"He's back. He showed up here about dark last night."

"Sure," Danny said. "I can use him." He smiled his smile. "Does he have something in particular he wants to do?"

"Whatever you need him to do," I said. "Anything. I want you to put him to work and keep him at it. All day every day."

"Sure."

"What he does for you, you can pay him for. What he does here or on his mother's place, we'll pay him for. But he'll be your hand. Ask what you need to ask of him. If he quits, he quits. Fire him if you have to."

"All right."

"Well, as soon as I can feed him his breakfast, I'll send him to you."

Danny went out to wait for Reuben. I called Virgie. When he had finished breakfast, I gave him Nathan's old work jacket and sent him up to the barn.

He has been at work with Danny and the other Branches every day since. Danny says he works hard, and he remembers enough of what Nathan taught him to work pretty well, though he has a lot to learn. Lyda has given him a haircut, on Danny's instructions, for fear that "all that hair would get wound up in something." He is living here with me. I give him breakfast and supper, he eats dinner with the Branches. Danny has started calling him "Virge."

He looks better. Confidence seems to be coming back into his eyes. All the necessary permissions have been given. He went to Louisville on his own permission and spent a Sunday with his mother. It has taken him too long to grow up, but he is young enough yet to make things well with himself and stand on his own feet and live his life. He has not told me where he has been or what he has done, and I have not asked, nor am I going to ask, nor do I want to know. All I want to know is that he is well and at work. So far, he is well and at work. The look of him has become a delight to me again.

Some day, maybe in a year or so, we will begin to know what this amounts to. After drugs and escape and whatever freedoms he has tried, can he stand what has got to be stood? Has he maybe learned the lesson he has tried at so much cost to teach his father?

I thought, anyhow, that something had begun to mend in him when he came in one evening after he had worked all day, cleaning a barn on the Feltner place with Fount Branch, who remembers things, and he told me from start to finish the story of Burley and Big Ellis and the disconnected steering wheel. He is too young to have any memory of Burley, and he told me the story as if I had never heard it. I pretended that I had never heard it, and we laughed.

When you have gone too far, as I think he did, the only mending is to come home. Whether he is equal to it or not, this is his chance.

Now and then the thought drifts into my mind that Virgie might actually prove himself a farmer and become worthy of the Feltner place and live there, and that Margaret, by his good favor, might end her days there, and all come somehow right at last. And then I let it drift on by. I let it come and go like a leaf floating on the river.

I know by now that the love of ghosts is not expectant, and I am coming to that. This Virgie of mine, this newfound "Virge," is the last care of my life, and I know the ignorance I must cherish him in. I must care for him as I care for a wildflower or a singing bird, no terms, no expectations, as finally I care for Port William and the ones who have been here with me. I want to leave here openhanded, with only the ancient blessing, "Good-bye. My love to you all."

24

Given

I am standing at the gate. Nathan has been salting the cattle down at the edge of the woods below the spring. Now he is walking back up the hill toward the house, toward me. He is walking in his thoughtful way with the salt bucket on his arm, looking around. He is whistling, as I know, over and over a piece of some old tune that will have the rhythm both of itself and of his breath.

I am watching him, but he has not yet seen me. And now he sees me. The expression on his face does not change, but now his intention has changed, he is walking toward me and nothing else. As he comes closer he smiles a little, still whistling. I know that when he comes to where I am he will give me a hug, and I want him to. I know how it is going to feel, the entire touch of him. He looks at me with a look I know. The shiver of the altogether given passes over me from head to foot.

Acknowledgments

Maybe I believed once that some day I would be able to write a novel by myself, and probably I thought I would be glad when that day came. It has never come. This novel, my seventh, has put me more in need of help than any of the previous six. And so my practice of this art has led, not to independence, but to debt and to gratitude—a better fate.

To clarify details of Virgil Feltner's and Nathan Coulter's involvement in World War II I found an ideal helper. Edward Coffman, military historian and my friend since our student days, addressed himself to my problems generously and precisely. He also contacted on my behalf his friend, Fletcher R. Veach, Jr., who commanded a company in the Battle of Okinawa, and Col. Veach responded graciously and usefully.

For my Chapter 21, "Okinawa," the principle sources are E. B. Sledge, *With the Old Breed;* George Feifer, *The Battle of Okinawa;* Donald O. Dencker, *Love Company;* and Sóetsu Yanagi, *The Unknown Craftsman.*

Tanya Berry listened sympathetically and critically to the chapters of the first draft as they were written, and she made the first typescript from my longhand. Tanya and Dave Charlton transcribed the much-edited typescript onto a computer disk, and suffered many further alterations and additions, all the while treating me and my book with wonderful kindness.

Don Wallis, yet once more, proved himself an illuminating critic and an indispensable friend.

Carol Berry, Mary Berry Smith, and Don Hall read the manuscript. Their kindness helped me, and the thought that they were reading my work made me more critical of it.

Trish Hoard and Jack Shoemaker, of Shoemaker & Hoard, gave me readings that encouraged me, changed my mind, and improved the book. Julie Wrinn, a conversable and exacting copy editor, did me many favors, large and small.

Chapter 20, "The Living," was published in the *Temenos Academy Review*, number 6.

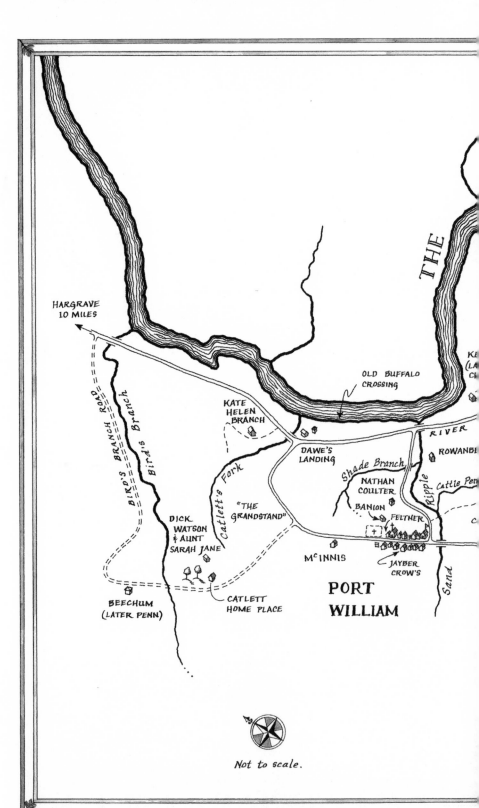

HARGRAVE
10 MILES

THE

OLD BUFFALO
CROSSING

KATE
HELEN
BRANCH

DAWE'S
LANDING

RIVER

ROWANBE

KE
(LA
Cl

BIRD'S BRANCH ROAD

Bird's Branch

Catlett's Fork

Shade Branch

NATHAN
COULTER

BANION

Ripple

Cattle Pen

"THE
GRANDSTAND"

DICK
WATSON
& AUNT
SARAH JANE

FELTNER

C

McINNIS

JAYBER
CROW'S

BEECHUM
(LATER PENN)

CATLETT
HOME PLACE

PORT
WILLIAM

Sand

Not to scale.

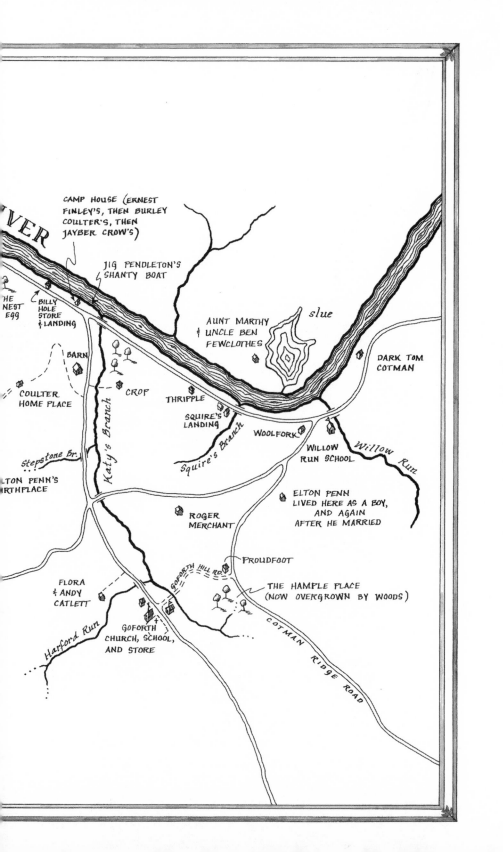

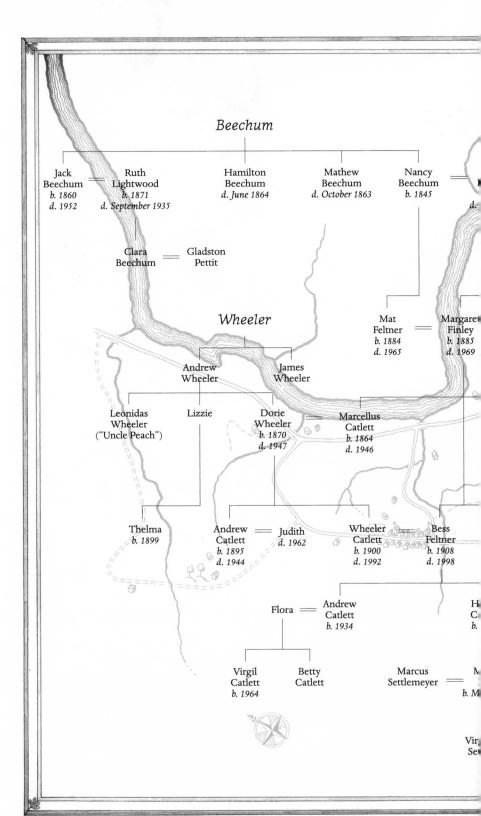

Beechum

Jack
Beechum
b. 1860
d. 1952
===
Ruth
Lightwood
b. 1871
d. September 1935

Hamilton
Beechum
d. June 1864

Mathew
Beechum
d. October 1863

Nancy
Beechum
b. 1845

d.

Clara
Beechum
===
Gladston
Pettit

Wheeler

Mat
Feltner
b. 1884
d. 1965
===
Margare
Finley
b. 1885
d. 1969

Andrew
Wheeler

James
Wheeler

Leonidas
Wheeler
("Uncle Peach")

Lizzie

Dorie
Wheeler
b. 1870
d. 1947
===
Marcellus
Catlett
b. 1864
d. 1946

Thelma
b. 1899

Andrew
Catlett
b. 1895
d. 1944
===
Judith
d. 1962

Wheeler
Catlett
b. 1900
d. 1992
===
Bess
Feltner
b. 1908
d. 1998

Flora
===
Andrew
Catlett
b. 1934

H
C
b.

Virgil
Catlett
b. 1964

Betty
Catlett

Marcus
Settlemeyer
===
N

b. M

Vir
Se

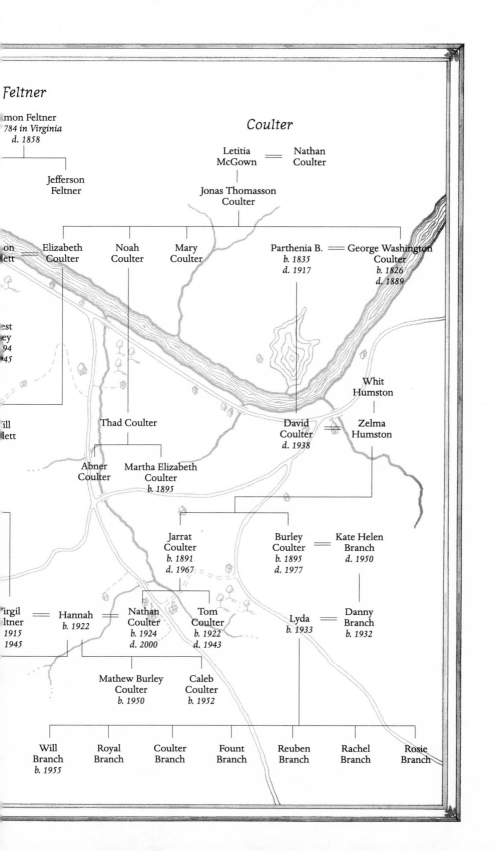

Feltner

...mon Feltner
...784 in Virginia
d. 1858

Coulter

Letitia McGown ═══ Nathan Coulter

Jefferson Feltner

Jonas Thomasson Coulter

...on ...lett ═══ Elizabeth Coulter   Noah Coulter   Mary Coulter   Parthenia B. b. 1835 d. 1917 ═══ George Washington Coulter b. 1826 d. 1889

...est ...ey ...94 ...45

...ill ...lett

Thad Coulter

Whit Humston

David Coulter d. 1938 ═══ Zelma Humston

Abner Coulter   Martha Elizabeth Coulter b. 1895

Jarrat Coulter b. 1891 d. 1967

Burley Coulter b. 1895 d. 1977 ═══ Kate Helen Branch d. 1950

...irgil ...ltner ...1915 ...1945 ═══ Hannah b. 1922 ═══ Nathan Coulter b. 1924 d. 2000   Tom Coulter b. 1922 d. 1943   Lyda b. 1933 ═══ Danny Branch b. 1932

Mathew Burley Coulter b. 1950   Caleb Coulter b. 1952

Will Branch b. 1955   Royal Branch   Coulter Branch   Fount Branch   Reuben Branch   Rachel Branch   Rosie Branch